COWBOYS, INDIANS, AND GUNFIGHTERS

*The Story of
the Cattle Kingdom*

COWBOYS, INDIANS, AND GUNFIGHTERS

*The Story of
the Cattle Kingdom*

ILLUSTRATED IN FULL COLOR AND BLACK AND WHITE

WITH PRINTS, PAINTINGS, PHOTOGRAPHS, AND MAP

ALBERT MARRIN

ATHENEUM   1993   NEW YORK

Maxwell Macmillan Canada
TORONTO

Maxwell Macmillan International
NEW YORK   OXFORD   SINGAPORE   SYDNEY

To the memory of my mother, Frieda Marrin

Atheneum
Macmillan Publishing Company
866 Third Avenue
New York, NY 10022

Maxwell Macmillan Canada, Inc.
1200 Eglinton Avenue East
Suite 200
Don Mills, Ontario M3C 3N1

Macmillan Publishing Company is part of the
Maxwell Communication Group of Companies.

First edition

Printed in the United States of America

10   9   8   7   6   5   4   3   2   1

The text of this book is set in 12/15 Bodoni Book.

Book design by Patrice Fodero
Book production by Daniel Adlerman

LIBRARY OF CONGRESS CATALOGING-IN-PUBLICATION DATA

Marrin, Albert.
Cowboys, Indians, and gunfighters: the story of the cattle kingdom / Albert Marrin.
p.   cm.
Includes bibliographical references (p. 185).
Summary: Describes life in the American West and the growth of the cattle industry, from the introduction of horses and cattle by the Spanish through the reign of the cattle barons in the late nineteenth century.
ISBN 0–689–31774–3
1. Ranch life—West (U.S.)—History—Juvenile literature.
2. Cattle trade—West (U.S.)—History—Juvenile literature.
3. Frontier and pioneer life—West (U.S.)—Juvenile literature.
4. West (U.S.)—Social life and customs—Juvenile literature.
[1. The West (U.S.)—History.   2. Frontier and pioneer life—West (U.S.)   3. Cattle trade—West (U.S.)   4. Cowboys.   5. Indians of North America—West (U.S.)]   I. Title.
F596.M28   1993
978—dc20   92–5727

It was still the Wild West in those days, the Far West . . . the West of the Indian and the buffalo hunter, the soldier and the cowpuncher. . . . It was a land of vast, silent spaces, of lonely rivers, and of plains where the wild game stared at the passing horseman. . . . We knew toil and hardship and hunger and thirst; and we saw men die violent deaths as they worked among the horses and cattle, or fought in evil feuds with one another; but we felt the beat of hardy life in our veins, and ours was the glory of work and the joy of living.

—Theodore Roosevelt, *An Autobiography*

Contents

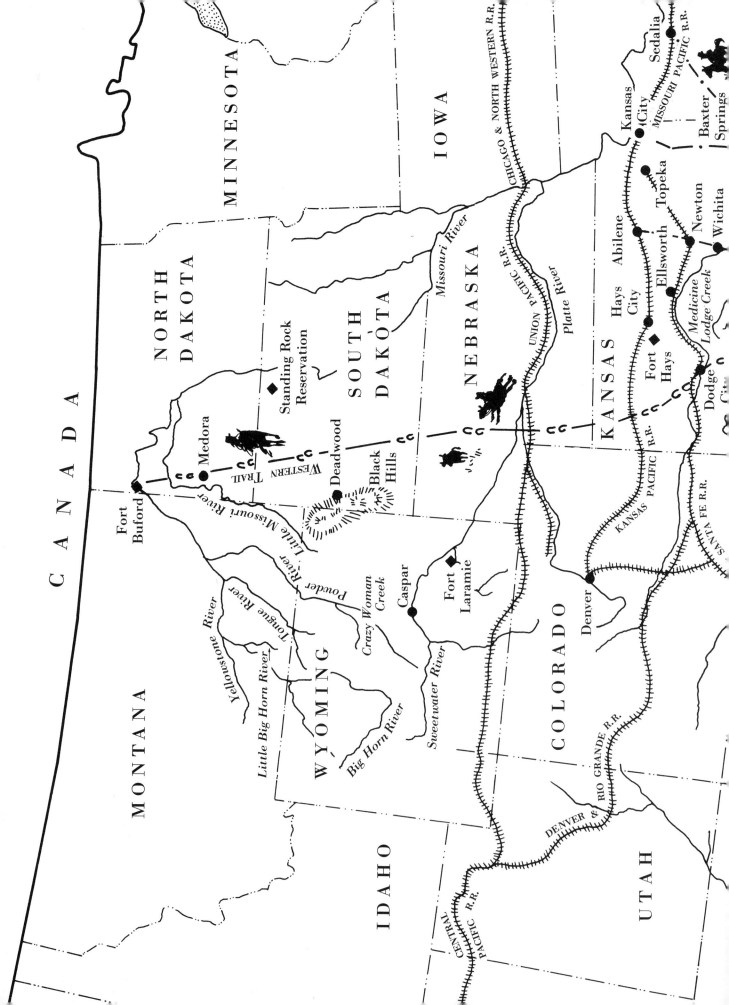

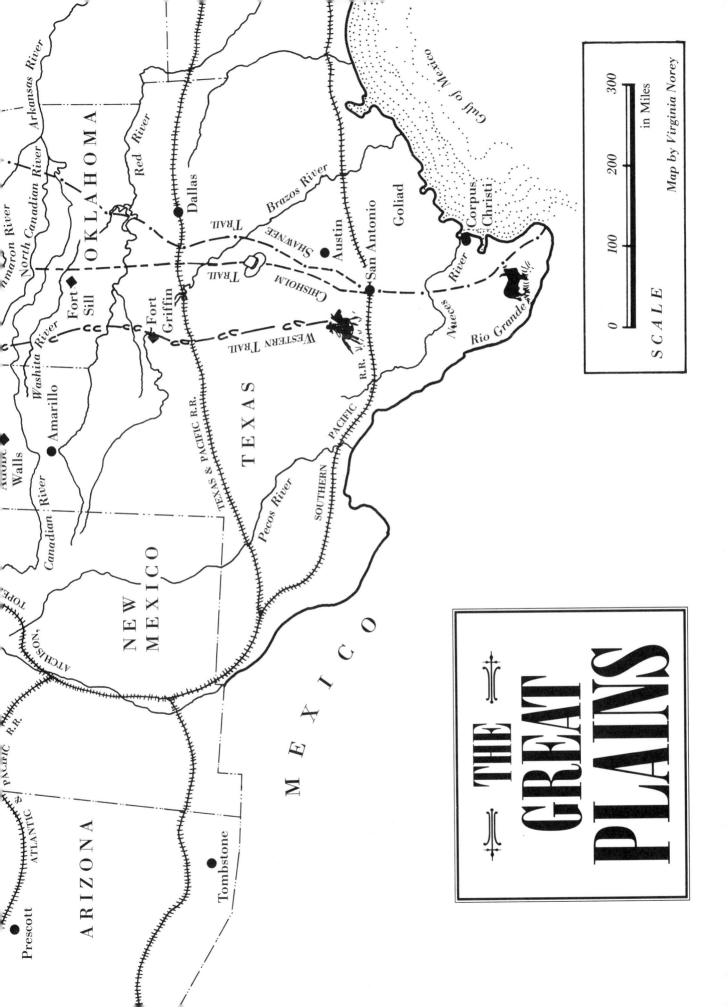

CHAPTER ONE

Noble Beasts of Spain

"Every beast in the forest is mine, and the cattle upon a thousand hills."

—*Psalms 50:10*

IN THE YEAR OF THE LORD 1493, AND THE TWENTY-FIFTH IN the reign of Their Catholic Majesties Ferdinand and Isabella, seventeen Spanish ships anchored off the northern coast of Hispaniola in the Caribbean Sea. On the deck of the flagship stood the fleet's commander, Christopher Columbus, Admiral of the Ocean Sea. His vessel, the *Santa María*, was the second of that name, the original having been lost during his first voyage the previous year. After it sank, Columbus put the crew ashore, ordering them to build a fort and await his return with reinforcements from home.

Columbus had kept his promise, only to find the fort in ruins; the sailors—thugs who robbed Indian villages and molested Indian women—had been massacred by the local people. The massacre put Columbus, a prudent man, on guard but in no way changed his plans. He had a mission, and it would go forward so long as he drew breath.

This second voyage was not merely an exploring expedition but the start of a permanent Spanish colony—the first of many, God willing. Aboard the vessels were twelve hundred sailors, soldiers, and settlers. The settlers had everything needed for a colony; indeed, they were to transplant the best of Spain to the New World. Belowdecks, stored in the darkened holds, were farm tools of every description, plus barrels of seeds and cuttings for the planting of wheat, onions, melons, radishes, grapevines, and sugarcane. Wooden cages held chickens, goats, sheep, and pigs. Best of all, the ships carried what people called the "noble beasts of Spain."

In their stalls on the upper decks, bracing themselves against the roll of the surf, were an unknown number of cattle and twenty-five horses, both stallions and mares. The cattle, from Andalusia, in southern Spain, were sturdy beasts with long horns and short tempers. Andalusia is cattle country—dry, flat, and covered with short grasses. For over a thousand years its people have bred cattle for food and for *la corrida*, "the bullfight."

The horses were the Spaniards' pride and joy. Small and lean, they seemed frail to those who did not know them. Descendants of Arabian horses brought by Muslim invaders seven centuries earlier, they were swift, hardy animals able to feed entirely on grass and get by with little water. Unlike the larger, grain-fed European horses, they had tremendous stamina and could go long distances without tiring.

Until the Spaniards arrived, cattle and horses were unknown in the Americas. Horses had existed there once. In prehistoric times, there had not only been horses, but woolly mammoths, saber-toothed tigers, and huge bears. Buffalo twice the size of today's animal roamed the plains of North America in vast herds.

All these creatures had vanished by the end of the last ice age, about twenty-five thousand years ago. This left the Native Americans with few animal helpers. There was the dog, for eating and carrying small bundles. The llama and alpaca were small South American camels prized for their meat and hair, which made excellent cloth. The guinea pig, turkey, and several types of duck were used for food. But the Indian had no animal that he could use for transportation. If he wanted to go anywhere fast, he ran. If he wanted to move a load, he moved it himself or, more likely, put it on his wife's back; women were expected to do the heavy work, leaving men free to hunt and fight. The wheel was unknown in the Americas, and there were no such things as carts or wheelbarrows.

The best sharpshooter in the New World. A buccaneer smokes his pipe while standing guard with his long, shovel-handled musket. Standing guard also are two half-wild dogs used to run down wild cattle and pigs.

The Spaniards turned the Indians' world topsy-turvy. Using Hispaniola as a base, they sent settlers to Cuba, Puerto Rico, and other Caribbean islands. And wherever the settlers went, they brought their noble beasts. In due time, a warm climate and plentiful food allowed them to multiply until they outnumbered the people. Even uninhabited islands were "seeded" with cattle so they could reproduce and provide food for passing ships. Sailors not only hunted them but learned to preserve their meat for long voyages. Meat was cut into thin, narrow strips and hung over racks near a fire made with green wood. The wood's dampness prevented the fire from becoming too hot, allowing the meat to cure in the smoke. The result was a tasty treat that could go months without spoiling. The meat took its name from the curing racks, called *bukans* by the Indians. Pirates soon learned the secret of *bukan*. French pirates called themselves *boucaniers*; Englishmen were known as buccaneers. Within a century of Columbus's arrival, French and English buccaneers were making fortunes by attacking Spanish treasure ships.

➤➤➤ **3**

Meantime, the West Indies developed a severe labor shortage. Spanish rule was so harsh that the Indians began to die out. Bartolomé de las Casas, a priest whose father had sailed on Columbus's second voyage, was ashamed of his countrymen. They had, he insisted, dishonored the proud Spanish name. In his *Very Brief Account of the Destruction of the Indies*, a book printed in 1552, he described some of their cruelties: "The Christians, with their horses and swords and lances, began to slaughter and practice strange cruelty among [the natives]. They penetrated into the country and spared neither children nor the aged . . . all of whom they ran through the body. . . ."[1]

Entire tribes were enslaved and then worked until they dropped from exhaustion. Runaways were tracked down and tortured to death as a lesson to their families. Those who failed to do a full day's work were thrown to packs of fierce hunting dogs; settlers called it *aperriamento*, "dogging" the Indians. As if this was not bad enough, smallpox and measles took thousands of lives each year. These European diseases were brought to the New World during Columbus's voyages. But while the Spaniards had built up an immunity to them over many centuries, the Indians were highly susceptible.

Even the noble beasts took their toll. As settlers spread across the islands, they seized Indian lands for pasture, reducing the amount of land available for agriculture. Since the Indians lived chiefly on fruits and vegetables, that meant hunger. Already weakened by overwork, they had no resistance to common infections like colds, let alone smallpox and measles. Once disease broke out in a village, it swept through it like wildfire. As a result, the population of Hispaniola fell from approximately two hundred thousand in 1493 to twenty-nine thousand within a generation. No wonder Indians said, "Where the Spaniard passes, no one remains to bury the dead."

By the early 1500s Spaniards were looking for new lands to conquer. Explorers had already heard rumors of mighty empires on the mainlands of North and South America. Although still few in numbers, the Spaniards were undaunted. Conquering "heathens," they believed, was a duty to God. Better yet, those heathens might have gold and silver, which made war all the

Opposite: This early native illustration shows, in figure 3, "dogging" the Indians. After the conquest of Mexico, the Indians were forced to become Christians and work for the Spaniards. In addition to guns, swords, and chains, the conquerors used fierce dogs to control the Indians.

➢➢➢ 5

more attractive. "We came here," a Spaniard admitted, "to serve God and also to get rich." With God's blessing, they believed, there was nothing to fear. If they succeeded, they would be rich. If they died, they would go straight to heaven.

The Spaniards and their noble beasts were the ideal fighting team. Some of the finest armies in history have been destroyed by hunger. Thanks to his cattle, however, hunger was seldom a problem for the Spanish soldier in the New World. As he advanced, he was followed by his cattle, a walking food supply. But it was his horses and his horsemanship that made him invincible. The Spaniard was the finest horseman in Europe. This is no exaggeration, simply a fact admitted by friend and foe alike. Even their language paid tribute to his ability. *Caballo* is Spanish for "horse"; a *caballero* is a horseman, nobleman, gentleman, or knight. Frenchmen borrowed the term, turning it into *chevalier*. Englishmen used the word *cavalier*, and cavaliers belonged to the cavalry.

Once the Spaniards set their sights on the mainland, nothing could turn them away. They began with the conquest of Mexico, followed by Peru and Central America. Early in 1519 Hernán Cortés landed in Mexico with 508 soldiers and 16 horses. Mexico at that time was ruled by the Aztec Empire, whose armies numbered in the tens of thousands. Gallant warriors, the Aztecs did not fight for the usual reasons. They had little interest in land or wealth but wanted victims to sacrifice to their gods. The gods, they believed, needed blood in order to attend to their duties. Without blood, they would grow tired and the forces of nature would not operate. The sun would not shine, the rain would not fall, and the universe would come to an end. To prevent this disaster, each year Aztec priests cut out the hearts of thousands of captives, offering them to their gods.

The gods were powerless against Cortés's men and horses. Although outnumbered by hundreds to one, mounted Spaniards defeated the Indians every time. Horses gave the Spaniards mobility, the ability to cover great distances and move around a battlefield quickly. Horses enabled them to wear armor, an important advantage, since soldiers in iron suits are not very effective on foot. Armor in turn protected them from the Indians' wooden and stone weapons.

Cortés's horses were the most important weapons in the conquest of Mexico, serving as the "tank corps" of his little army.

Battles followed a set pattern. As war drums throbbed, the Indians massed under their banners of colorful bird feathers. The Spanish cavalry, protected by foot soldiers on either side, spurred their mounts and gave their war cry. *"Santiago! Santiago y a ellos!"* they'd shout, calling upon Spain's patron saint. "Saint James! Saint James and at them!"

Indians, who had never seen this before, became terrified. The size of the animals, and their obedience to their riders, seemed supernatural. Surely horses and riders were demons, they thought. Those who stood their ground learned what those "demons" could do at close quarters. A man and horse weighed about a ton. Traveling at twenty miles an hour, they struck with terrific force. Anyone who fell under the hooves was crushed. The riders lunged with their spears or, leaning over, swung their swords with all their might. Indians fell, stabbed through the heart; others were split from shoulder to hip or had their heads lopped off by the sharp blades. After the battle, the heads were stuck on wooden poles to spread fear among the survivors.

Never were the lives of animals so precious. To the Spaniards, the loss of a horse was reckoned as the loss of a friend. Ironclad warriors wept over their fallen "comrades." Bernal Díaz del

Castillo, the soldier-author whose *Discovery and Conquest of Mexico* is an eyewitness account, gives the name of every horse and describes it in minute detail. "It was the greatest grief to think upon the horses, and the valiant soldiers we lost," he recalled years later. Notice that the horses came first, the men second in his thoughts. Although the Spaniards had fourteen light cannons, these were not nearly as important as their beloved horses.

In February 1521, six months before the fall of the Aztec capital, the future Mexico City, a vessel arrived at the coast. Aboard was a mixed lot of cattle—bulls and cows—sent from Hispaniola by Gregorio de Villalobos. Little is known of Villalobos except that he became lieutenant governor of Mexico and that he started a ranch near Vera Cruz on the Gulf of Mexico. Villalobos's *rancho* was so successful that others followed his example. During the next few years, so many cattle and horses were sent from Hispaniola that cattlemen there protested. Their protests were heard by the governor, who decreed the death

European animals arrive in Mexico, about the year 1519. Until Hernán Cortés came, the Aztec Indians had never seen horses, cattle, or pigs, none of which were native to the New World.

penalty for anyone sending livestock to the mainland. But the decree frightened no one, least of all Cortés and his soldiers. Cortés himself went into the cattle business. After the conquest, he built a great ranch on lands taken from the Aztecs. He called it Cuernavaca—"Cow Horn." The Hispaniola trade ended only in the late 1520s, by which time Mexican herds were growing beyond their owners' wildest dreams.

Cattle flourished in Mexico, the herds doubling every fifteen months. By the 1570s, some ranches had 150,000 head of cattle; 20,000 was considered a small herd and its owner a man of no importance. After touring the country, the French explorer Samuel de Champlain reported ranches "stretching endlessly and everywhere covered with an infinite number of cattle."[2]

Cattle brought prosperity and comfort to the conquerors. Meat prices fell; a whole side of beef cost but a few copper coins. This was true luxury, since the average European thought himself lucky to have meat once a month, and that usually so spoiled that it needed spices to mask the taste. Cattle also provided valuable raw materials. Cowhide was turned into leather, as useful then as plastic and metal are today. Clothing, rope, drinking cups, water bags, harnesses, shields, and the padded vests worn by foot soldiers were all made of leather. Hooves and horns could be boiled in water for the glue they contained. Hair was used for padding and mixed into plaster to give it added strength. Fat, or tallow, could be eaten or made into soap. Tallow's most important use, however, was for candles. Before the electric light, buildings were lit by candles or oil lamps. Without candles, each two feet long by five inches thick, miners could not work underground. And without mining, Spain would not get the gold and silver to pay for its wars in Europe. Candles were so cheap in Mexico that even the poor could afford them. Before candles, they simply went to bed at sunset.

Specially trained workers were needed to handle the cattle. Since the conquerors saw themselves as masters, not workers, physical labor was beneath their dignity. Tending cattle was for the lowly, for the Indian. Thus the *vaquero*, or Mexican "cowboy," was born.

The original vaqueros were slaves. After defeating the Aztecs, Cortés marched lines of chained prisoners in front of bonfires.

As each man's turn came, a blacksmith drew a branding iron from the fire and burned the letter *G* for *guerra*, "war," on his lips and cheeks. Painful as it was, branding was not unusual, nor was it regarded as cruel—by Europeans. The custom of branding one's property goes back thousands of years. Ancient Chinese and Egyptians branded their farm animals. Greeks burned a delta (Δ), the fourth letter of their alphabet, on slaves' cheeks; Romans burned criminals with the letter *F*, meaning *fur* ("thief") in Latin. Spaniards branded slaves and cattle with letters or complicated designs. Cortés's personal brand was three Christian crosses in gratitude for God's allowing him to conquer Mexico.

Cortés kept one-fifth of the slaves for himself and gave the rest to his followers for their ranches. These vaqueros worked on foot, since the law forbade Indians to own horses or learn to ride. Horses were weapons of war, and Spaniards did not want them to fall into the wrong hands. But as the cattle multiplied, it became clear that they could not be managed on foot. At first a handful of trusted slaves, then freeborn Indians, were taught to ride. They took to the saddle easily, gaily, for riding brought self-respect. A horseman, however poor, was a proud person. He rose above the crowd, who ate his dust as he galloped past. Like the Spaniard, the Indian became bowlegged from countless hours in the saddle; and, like him, he never walked if he could ride. To this day the vaquero is the equal of any horseman on earth.

It was a hard life. Home for the vaquero was an open-sided wooden shack roofed with cowhide. His bed was the ground, with only a straw mat between him and Mother Earth. Food was tortillas, flat cakes made by mixing cornmeal and water, fried in tallow. Another favorite was tamales, steamed cornmeal dough filled with meat and seasoned with hot chili peppers.

Vaquero clothing was simple and suited to the job. Each man wore a shirt and pants of raw, undyed cotton. A serape, a brightly colored woolen shawl worn as a cape, kept him warm. A wide-brimmed hat, or sombrero, protected him from the sun's heat and glare. Its name comes from the word *sombra*, Spanish for "shade"; the sombrero is literally a "shade maker."

The vaquero's tools were as practical as his clothes. Although he went barefoot, he wore a pair of iron spurs to help control

Spanish bit brand

his horse. Attached to each spur was a rowel, a rotating disk ranging in size from that of a silver dollar to a teacup saucer. Wicked things studded with sharp points, rowels could scrape a horse's sides raw. In addition, two devices were used for catching cattle. If the animal was to be butchered, the vaquero carried a long pole tipped with *la luna*, "the moon," a blade shaped like a half-moon, the sharpened curve facing outward. He would ride up to the animal and cut the muscle of its right hind leg, sending it crashing to the ground. Dismounting, he straddled its back and drove a dagger into its brain, killing it instantly. But if it was to be captured for branding, *la reata*, "the rope," was used. The vaquero's rope was made of thin strips of rawhide woven into a single strand with a loop at the end. Normally, a reata was sixty feet long, although some were twice that. A true artist, using a long rope, could catch a running animal sixty feet away. One vaquero roped a low-flying eagle!

More vaqueros were needed after silver was discovered in northern Mexico. To feed the miners, herds of cattle were driven to ranches set up near Durango. Yet this was only the beginning. Hoping to find even more silver, the Spaniards pushed farther, into what would later be United States territory. In 1598, they reached New Mexico, home of the Pueblo Indians, a peaceful farming people who lived in villages built into the sides of cliffs. After conquering the Pueblos, the Spaniards founded missions to convert them to Christianity. In order to pay their expenses, the mission priests, or padres, raised cattle and sold their hides in Mexico. Although the padres were excellent horsemen, there were never enough of them. They lost no time in teaching trusted Indians to be vaqueros.

Almost a century later, in 1689, other Spaniards crossed the Rio Grande, or "Great River." Moving in a northeasterly direction, they met a band of Hasinai, a tribe that lived by planting corn and vegetables. When asked to identify themselves, the Hasinai cried, *"Teychas! Teychas!"*—"Friends! Friends!" The Spaniards called them Tejas, which they pronounced "Te-has." Settlers from the United States later called themselves Texans.

Missions were also founded in Texas, two eventually growing into San Antonio and Goliad, its chief towns. And, as be-

An early map shows missions founded by Spanish priests.

fore, the noble beasts followed close behind. The Spaniards had never fenced their grazing lands in the New World. Animals ran free, to be rounded up as needed. Some wandered off and were lost, but this was not a serious problem, since they were so plentiful. Besides, there were few places for them to hide, and they could easily be rounded up. But Texas was so vast that an animal, once lost, might never be seen again. Many cattle that wandered off hid in the dense brush that grew along the rivers and streams of East Texas. There they multiplied, forming the wild herds that became the basis of the American cattle kingdom.

Horses, too, escaped in large numbers. When Father Morfi, a Spanish missionary, visited the area between the Rio Grande and the Nueces River in 1777, he could scarcely believe his eyes. Horses were so abundant, he wrote, "that their trails make the country, utterly uninhabited by people, look as if it were the most populated in the world."[3] His countrymen called them *mesteños*; that is, "homeless ones," or "strays." Their descendants, known as mustangs, still roam parts of the American West.

The Spanish settlements, however, never grew as rapidly as their herds. By 1800 there were only three thousand settlers in the whole of Texas. In spite of the country's size, they were locked into east Texas, an area of abundant rainfall, rolling hills, and forests of hickory and pine. They dared not venture too far to the west or northwest. There lay a world of mystery and danger: the world of the Great Plains.

The Great Plains of North America reach southward from Canada to Mexico and westward from the Mississippi River to the Rocky Mountains—an area of 1.3 million square miles, 44 percent of the continental United States. Compared to Europe, it is larger than the combined territory of the British Isles, France, Germany, Norway, Sweden, Denmark, Finland, Holland, Belgium, Austria, Italy, Spain, and Portugal. But, unlike these countries, with their mountains and valleys, lakes and forests, all of the plains is the same.

As the name indicates, the plains are flat, curving gently with the curvature of the earth. The early explorers, all European-born, were never comfortable there. In 1540 Francisco Vásquez de Coronado led an army across the plains to what is now Kansas. The country was so smooth and featureless, one of his soldiers reported, that if you looked at a buffalo in the distance, the sky could be seen between its legs. Even when you came closer, you could not see the ground behind the animal. "The land," he wrote, "is like the inside of a bowl, so that wherever a man stands he is surrounded by the sky at the distance of a crossbow shot."[4]

The Great Plains is the land of the big sky. The dome of it comes down to meet the earth, forming a circle around the horizon. Since there are few landmarks, it is easy to get lost. Coronado's men would leave camp to hunt buffalo, lose their way, and never be seen again.

Plains weather is often harsh and unpredictable. Summers can be oven-hot, with temperatures of a hundred degrees for weeks at a time. In winter, winds known as northers sweep down from Canada, sending temperatures to fifty degrees below zero. Texans tell tall tales about their weather, yet these have a kernel of truth. It is so changeable, one fellow grumbled, that "when I saw the tumbleweeds jump away from the north fence like a jackrabbit leaving a nest of yellowjackets, I knew that a norther had hit. By morning it was so cold that I had to run backward to spit."[5] In addition, the plains have their share of cloudbursts, hailstorms, lightning strikes, tornadoes, and prairie fires. The wind howls constantly, and people have been driven insane by the noise.

Above all, the plains are dry. The land between the eastern slopes of the Rockies and the hundredth meridian, an imaginary line passing through the center of the plains, averages less than twenty inches of rain a year. This explains why the plains are labeled the Great American Desert on maps of the 1830s and 1840s. Except for scattered cottonwoods growing along the riverbanks, they are treeless, covered only by grass and, in the Southwest, by prickly pear, thornbushes, and mesquite, a scrubby, twisted tree with a massive root system.

Grass is life in these parts. Plains animals lived on grass or on those that feed on grass. Pronghorn antelope bounded across the countryside. Weighing less than a hundred pounds, the pronghorn was built for speed and endurance. With its long, muscular legs, large heart, and oversize lungs, it could travel for hours at thirty miles an hour; no coyote or wolf could catch a healthy pronghorn. Flocks of wild turkey extended for miles. Prairie dogs, a type of ground squirrel that barks like a small dog, lived in underground "cities." One city in Texas covered twenty-five thousand square miles and contained an estimated four hundred million inhabitants. But the lords of the plains were the American bison, or buffalo. Resembling large, shaggy cattle, they trampled deep trails while moving from one feeding ground to another. Some buffalo trails later became wagon roads and, in time, paved highways. The buffalo's encounter with the white man nearly drove them to extinction, a tragedy we shall examine later.

Indians had lived on the plains for centuries. On the southern plains, the major tribes were the Comanche and Kiowa; the Sioux, Cheyenne, Crow, Arapaho, and Blackfeet lived on the northern plains. Though differing in language and customs, these tribes had several things in common. All were warrior peoples who roamed the plains, eking out a living by gathering wild berries and hunting the buffalo. It was a hard life, because with only their legs for transportation, they could never keep up with the herds. This was especially true in winter, the Indians' worst season. Each winter they braced for the "starving time," days or weeks when hunters returned empty-handed. Individuals were now sacrificed to the common good. Old people were abandoned and left to die so that the young might survive; after all, they were the tribe's future. Infants, however, might be put to death to spare them the agony of starvation.

Then came the horse. The Plains tribes began to get horses about the year 1650. Spanish missionaries had taught Pueblo Indians to ride and herd cattle. These vaqueros were often mistreated, forced to work long hours and whipped if they failed to attend church regularly. In retaliation, each year scores of vaqueros fled to the buffalo hunters on the plains. To make themselves welcome, they brought gifts of stolen horses, along with their skills as horsemen. They taught their friends to ride and to capture and tame mustangs. As the Indian herds grew, they in turn traded their older mounts to their neighbors and taught them to ride. In this way Spanish horses spread from south to north. By 1770 all the tribes from Texas to Canada had become "horse Indians."

The horse was no ordinary creature to the Plains Indians. They gave it a noble name, a religious name: Súñka Wakan, "Spirit Dog." They saw it, like the buffalo, as a gift from Wakan Taka, the "Great Spirit," as a token of his love. Their eastern brothers, forest peoples like the Mohawk and Iroquois, had little use for horses; they lived in permanent villages, planted corn and squash, and hunted small animals. But the horse changed the Plains Indians' entire way of life, bringing about a golden age that is remembered with pride to this very day.

The Native American and the horse were made for each other. He was a natural rider at home in the saddle, graceful, proud, and handsome. The horse enabled him to travel fast and far. Now he could go anywhere, keeping close to the buffalo herds and killing all he needed. That gave him more of everything—more food, more clothes, more tepees, more weapons.

The coming of the horse, or "Spirit Dog," completely changed the life of the Plains Indians. Here, Kiowa braves hunt buffalo on horseback.

Traveling from place to place was no longer a hardship. A horse could move heavy loads on a travois, a platform fastened between wooden poles and dragged along the ground. And since there were no more starving times, his numbers increased; indeed, an expert hunter could afford two or three wives and a large brood of children. In short, the horse made the Plains Indians wealthy.

It also made them masters in their own land. No other Indians were able to resist the whites so successfully and for so long a time. The eastern tribes, though gallant warriors, fought the whites at a disadvantage. Living in permanent farming villages, they made easy targets for raiding parties. In order to defeat them, the whites had only to burn their homes, destroy their crops, and send them fleeing into the wilderness. George Washington, for example, earned his Iroquois name, "Town Destroyer." During the American Revolution, he ordered villages to be burned in retaliation for Indian aid to the British.

It was different in the West. For two centuries, the Plains tribes blocked the whites' advance across the continent. This

was not because they were stronger or braver than their eastern cousins. It was because their country was open and the horse enabled them to move around it quickly. They did not have to fight on the enemy's terms. If an enemy was too strong, they leaped into their saddles and sped away. They fought only when they had the advantage. A war party would swoop down on a wagon train or outpost, kill the whites, steal their goods, and be gone before the enemy got over their surprise. If the whites came after them, they split into tiny groups, vanishing into the vastness of the plains.

The finest Plains horsemen were the Comanche. There were five major Comanche bands, each with its own chief: Honey Eaters, Those Who Turn Back, Antelope, Buffalo Eaters, and Root Eaters. George Catlin, an American artist, visited them in the 1830s to paint their pictures and study their way of life. He wrote in his 1844 book *North American Indians*:

Here, a horse draws a travois, a device made of wooden poles, for moving belongings and often children and old people.

> The Comanche are in stature, rather low, and . . . in their move-
> ments, they are rather heavy and ungraceful; and on their feet

➤➤➤ **17**

This old print from *Harper's* magazine shows Mexican ranchers battling Plains Indians on horseback.

one of the most unattractive and slovenly-looking races of Indians that I have ever seen. . . . A Comanche on his feet is out of his element, and comparatively almost as awkward as a monkey on the ground, without a limb or a branch to cling to; but the moment he lays his hand upon his horse, his *face*, even, becomes handsome, and he gracefully flies away like a different being. . . .[6]

They were, quite simply, the finest riders on earth. Everyone who met the Comanche admired their horsemanship. "He rides like a Comanche" was the highest compliment one Texan could pay another.

Horses were precious to the Comanche, and they would do anything to get them. Stealing was a normal part of their life. The Comanche compared himself to the snake; in sign language he made a wriggling movement with his index finger, indicating that he was "sly" as a snake. He stole horses for both fun and profit. A really good time, because it also involved danger, was stealing from other Indians. True, if caught he expected to be tortured to death. But danger only added spice to the game. A lone Comanche could crawl into a camp where an enemy war party lay asleep, each brave with his horse tied to his wrist, cut the rope six feet from a sleeper's wrist, and take his horse without waking anyone. A successful horse thief proved his courage, winning the respect of his people. The world's champion thief, however, stole a sleeping woman from her husband's side without waking either!

The Comanche were the most feared warriors of the plains. They lived for war, enjoying it as the ultimate adventure. Wherever they went, they waged war without mercy, expecting no mercy in return. Their very name reveals the hatred other tribes had for them. It was given them by the Ute, one of their favorite targets. Comanche comes from *Komantcia*, Ute for the "People Who Fight Us All the Time." Even the Apache, no slouches when it came to war, were terrified of them. About the year 1740, the Comanche drove the Apache off the plains, forcing them into the deserts and mountains of New Mexico.

Skill with weapons combined with trick riding made the Comanche the terror of the plains. George Catlin described the Comanche warrior in all his glory:

Amongst their feats of riding, there is one that has astonished me more than anything of the kind I have ever seen, or expect to see, in my life: a stratagem of war, learned and practiced by every young man in the tribe; by which he is able to drop his body upon the side of his horse and the instant he is passing, effectively screened from his enemies' weapons as he lies in a horizontal position behind the body of his horse, with his heel hanging over the horse's back; by which he has the power of throwing himself up again, and changing to the other side of the horse if necessary. In this wonderful condition, he will hang whilst his horse is at fullest speed, carrying him with his bow and shield, and also his long lance of fourteen feet in length, all or either of which he will wield upon his enemy as he passes; rising and throwing his arrows over the horse's back, or with equal success under the horse's neck. This astonishing feat . . . appears to be the result of magic, rather than of skill acquired by practice. . . .[7]

Catlin later found that this was not magic at all. Each brave had woven a loop of buffalo hair into his horse's mane. When he wanted to "disappear," he simply dropped over one side,

Plains Indian riders would hang over one side of their mounts so as not to expose themselves as targets to the enemy. Often, though, the Americans simply shot down the horses, which *were* good targets. A drawing by Frederic Remington.

holding on with a heel hooked over its back and an elbow hooked into the loop.

The full moon of summer—the "Comanche moon"—struck terror into the hearts of their enemies. Indians as well as whites begged their gods to spare them from the Comanche scourge. Comanche raiders thought nothing of riding a thousand miles to strike at an enemy. War parties galloped into central Mexico, killing, looting, and taking prisoners as they went. A successful raid brought as many as three thousand fine horses.

Human beings were another form of "loot." Young children, stolen from their families, were raised as Comanche. There was no racial discrimination, and even whites were treated as equals.

If they were boys, their adoptive fathers taught them to ride, hunt, and fight. When they came of age, they married Comanche girls; indeed, they might even become war chiefs. Captured girls were raised to be Comanche wives; adult women were either enslaved or married to their captors. In this the Comanche were not alone. Plains tribes usually adopted captives to replace people killed in war or lost through disease. Adult male prisoners, however, were killed outright or saved for a lingering death by torture.

In July 1769, the *San Carlos* put to sea from Mexico under a bright Comanche moon. Later called the *"Mayflower* of the West,"* she carried Spanish colonists, farm tools, and seven head of cattle. Sailing north, along the Pacific coast, she headed for California, a thousand miles away. The "California" of legend was an island located "very near the earthly paradise." The real California, Spanish California, could have been paradise itself. Its mild climate and rich soil were ideal for a colony. Labor would be no problem, for there were plenty of "tame" Indians to do the work. To save the Indians' souls while they worked, the Spaniards intended to set up missions and *presidios*— "forts"—along the coast.

The *San Carlos* anchored at a place called San Diego Bay, where Father Junípero Serra, the expedition's leader, built his first mission. Gradually, a string of missions grew up along the coastline, each fourteen leagues (about forty-two miles), or one day's journey on horseback, from the other. In time, some of these would become prosperous towns: San Diego, Santa Barbara, Monterey, San Jose. The most famous were the "City of Angels," or Los Angeles, and Yerba Buena ("Good Herb"), better known as San Francisco.

The missions met their food needs from their own lands. At the San Jose Mission, a field one mile square produced enough wheat to feed the residents for a year; grapes grown in its vineyards became wine and *aguardiente*, "fire water," a strong liquor. And, as usual, missions raised cattle to pay their expenses. Within a generation, mission herds numbered in the hundreds of thousands. At the San Gabriel Mission, one of the largest, Indian vaqueros tended 150,000 cattle, 20,000 horses, and 40,000 sheep. In time, anyone willing to build a house could get free land from the Mexican government and become a rancher. Ranching became the Californians' only occupation; so much so that five million hides were exported between 1800 and 1848. Nearly all of these, plus millions of gallons of tallow, went to the United States.

Cattle raising provided a high standard of living—for the ranchers. Californians manufactured nothing. Any article they needed was imported from the United States, brought by ship around the tip of South America. It was a dangerous voyage, lasting two years round-trip, but worth the efforts. The Yankee peddlers charged many times what their goods were worth in the East. Upon arriving at a town, the merchant dropped anchor and set up a market ashore. He offered tea, coffee, sugar, spices, hardware, cloth, clothing, boots, shoes, jewelry, furniture, and countless other items, including Chinese fireworks. Customers would pay any price, without complaint, even if overcharged. So long as they had cattle and Indian vaqueros to care for them, there would always be more "California bank notes" (hides) tomorrow.

Californians were easygoing, happy-go-lucky people. Unlike the tough-minded Yankees, they were content to eat well, work little, and enjoy life to the fullest. Richard Henry Dana, an author who went to sea as a young man, visited them in 1835–1836 aboard the ship *Pilgrim*. His experiences are re-

Two scenes from early California. The Mexicans, who settled the area in the 1700s, were magnificent riders and went everywhere on horseback. Here is a landowner and his foreman.

corded in *Two Years before the Mast,* an American classic. Although cattle were the Californians' wealth, horses, Dana noted, were their joy. Horses were the cheapest things in California; a good mount cost three or four dollars. Just as today's Californians would be lost without cars, their ancestors relied upon their horses.

> There are no stables to keep [horses] in, but they are allowed to run wild and graze wherever they please, being branded, and having long leather ropes, called "lassos," attached to their necks and dragging along behind them, by which they can be easily taken. The men usually catch one in the morning, throw a saddle and bridle upon him, and use him for the day, and let him go at night, catching another the next day. When they go on long journeys, they ride one horse down, and catch another, throw the saddle and bridle upon him, and after riding him down, take a third, and so on to the end of the journey. There are probably no better riders in the world. [Dana never saw the Comanche.] They get upon a horse when only four or five years old, their little legs not long enough to come half way over his sides; and may almost be said to keep on him until they have grown to him.[8]

Californians acted as if anything that could not be done on horseback wasn't worth doing. They gladly rode a hundred miles to attend a wedding or just to say hello to a friend. If they needed

At left, a woman rider joins the men. Respectable ladies never straddled a horse but rode sidesaddle.

firewood, they lassoed a bundle and dragged it home. A gentleman who wanted to kill someone caught his victim with *la reata* and dragged him to death along the ground. Knives and guns were undignified weapons.

Men were eager to show off their riding skills. A *rodeo*, or "roundup," was held once a week to obtain fresh meat. *Matanzas*, or "large-scale slaughters," were held to obtain hides and tallow. When the work was done, ranchers and vaqueros celebrated with sporting contests. Horse races were not merely tests of speed, but of split-second timing and control. Horsemen would gallop toward a rope stretched across the ground, then halt their mounts the moment they touched it; failure meant being pitched off the horse headfirst. Other contests involved "snatches" of various sorts. A group riding at top speed would lean from the saddle to grab coins off the ground. Or they played *el carrera del gallo*, "coursing the rooster." A rooster was buried with only its head exposed while riders tried to pull it free. If it was lucky, the poor rooster came out of the ground with its feathers ruffled. Usually, however, its head came off in the rider's hand.

The highlight of any rodeo matched riders against ferocious animals, and animals against one another. Bullfighting was a popular sport, but with a difference. Unlike in Spain, where a man met a bull on foot with a cape and sword, Californians fought on horseback without weapons. In *la corrida de toro*, "baiting the bull," a bull was let loose in a fenced area while people on the sidelines provoked it to a killing frenzy. Then the rider came forward. His object was not to kill, but to get as close as possible without touching the bull's horns. The most daring riders would "tail the bull"; that is, come on at full gallop, grab its tail, and jerk it to one side, flipping the bull over. That stunned the animal, perhaps even broke its neck. A fellow who could tail the bull was always a favorite of the *señoritas*.

Fighting a grizzly bear was the supreme test of courage for horse and rider. Grizzlies were plentiful in old California, feeding off the cattle remains left on the matanza grounds. Two riders would catch a grizzly with their ropes, one by the neck and the other by a hind leg. Then they spurred their mounts, pulling in opposite directions until the bear died. Sometimes the grizzly was spared for a more horrible contest. A bear and a bull were let loose in a pen, or one of the bear's hind legs was tied to one of the bull's forelegs. Men, women, and children shouted and made bets on the outcome. Californians were avid gamblers; small children even bet the buttons on their clothes until not one was left to hold them together. Occasionally, these "sports" ended in human tragedy, as when a rider fell into the pen during a bear-and-bull contest. The grizzly, a reporter noted, turned away from the bull and ran "straight at the man, striking one paw at his head. The man was literally scalped, and in a second more the grizzly had torn the man into a horrible mass."[9]

But while Californians were enjoying their way of life, events were taking place far to the east, in Texas. Although no one could know it then, those events would change the lives of five peoples—Americans, Mexicans, Californians, Texans, Indians—drastically and forever.

CHAPTER TWO

Land of the Longhorn

Other states are carved or born;
Texas grew from hide and horn.

Other states are long or wide;
Texas is a shaggy hide.

Dripping blood and crumpled hair,
Some gory giant flung it there,

Laid the head where valleys drain,
Stretched its rump along the plain.

Other soil is full of stones;
Texans plow up cattle bones. . . .

—Berta Hart Nance

THE UNITED STATES WAS A YOUNG, RESTLESS NATION. EVEN
before it had won its independence in 1783, pioneers had begun
their westward trek, across the Alleghenies into Kentucky and
Tennessee. Independence only encouraged the westward movement. The future, for countless Americans, lay beyond the settled areas along the Atlantic coast. Land—cheap, abundant,
fertile—was to be had in the West. There people could, through
hard work, build better lives than their forefathers had ever
known.

By 1800 Mexico was feeling American pressure. Adventurers, called "filibusters," crossed from United States soil into Texas to capture mustangs. The lucky ones did well, selling their catch at top prices. The unlucky were shot by Spanish troops, who left their bodies to the buzzards and coyotes. One group was captured, brought to Mexico City, and ordered to roll dice to decide their fate. The losers went before a firing squad; the winners were freed only after years in prison. Nevertheless, Americans continued to cross into Texas illegally.

The pressure increased after the Louisiana Purchase. In 1803 President Thomas Jefferson bought the Louisiana Territory[1] from France for fifteen million dollars, or three cents an acre, doubling the nation's size. From 1803 to 1806, Meriwether Lewis and William Clark explored the new lands, over eight hundred thousand square miles between the Mississippi and the Rockies. It was a difficult journey, but they proved it possible to reach the Pacific Ocean by traveling overland. Their discoveries fired people's imaginations. Americans began to speak about Manifest Destiny, the idea that God wanted them to create an "empire of liberty" from the Atlantic to the Pacific, from Canada into Mexico.

Mexico lacked both the power and population to control so large an area as Texas. There were so few Mexicans in Texas that the Americans had only to appear in large numbers and it would be theirs for the taking. Thus, in 1821, after winning its own independence from Spain, Mexico decided to build a human barrier against invasion. And the way to do that was to offer Americans free land in return for settling in Texas and becoming loyal Mexican citizens.

Americans poured into Texas by the thousands. They were a mixed lot, people from all walks of life. Some were shady characters anxious to keep a step ahead of the law. If one day the sheriff was looking for someone, the next he might find G.T.T. (GONE TO TEXAS) chalked on the front door. There were also adventurers like Davy Crockett, the legendary frontiersman, and Jim Bowie, inventor of the knife that bears his name. A murderous weapon, the bowie knife was known as the "genuwine Arkansas toothpick." The majority, however, were ordinary folks from the Southern states, some of whom brought slaves to work on cotton plantations near the coast. The largest group, led by Stephen F. Austin, settled along the Brazos River, where they built the town of San Felipe de Austin—Austin for short.

Although farmers for the most part, they took a keen interest in raising cattle. Only a fool would have done otherwise. The Mexican government, to encourage settlement, offered twenty-five times as much land to ranchers as to farmers. Settlers who went in only for farming received 177 acres. That was a lot back home, but in Texas it seemed like a grain of sand on a beach. However, if they promised to raise cattle, they received 4,438 acres, because cattle needed plenty of room for grazing. The offer was too good to refuse, and so, from the beginning, Texans were cattlemen.

Settlers already had cattle to put on their land. When they went west, they brought thousands of head to be used by their families for milk and meat. These were mainly British breeds, but after they arrived in Texas they changed in ways no one could have predicted. On the unfenced range they, like the Spanish cattle before them, roamed freely. Naturally, many wandered off and mingled with the wild herds. The result was a new breed, one that combined the best features of each. It is known as the Texas longhorn.

The longhorn was an amazing beast. Lanky and swaybacked, with big ears and long legs, it varied in color from black to red, yellow, white, and spotted. It weighed from eight hundred pounds for youngsters to twice that for ten-year-olds. Its most noticeable feature, of course, was its horns. They *were* something to see—and fear. On average they measured three to five feet from tip to tip. Mature bulls often had horns measuring six feet across; the longest on record is eight feet, one and three-eighths inches. The longhorn's long horns became part of Texas folklore. An old song tells how the daughter of a "muley," a cow that had lost its horns, made up for her mother's failing:

> Old Joe Clark has got a cow—
> She was muley born.
> It takes a jaybird forty-eight hours
> To fly from horn to horn.

Stephen F. Austin led settlers to the Brazos River, where they built the town of San Felipe de Austin.

A mature Texas longhorn bull weighed about a ton. Few of these animals remain today, and those that do are kept as curiosities, not as food sources.

The longhorn had what ranchers called "cow sense." Not that it was an intelligent creature; far from it. Rather, it was adapted to surviving in the wild. Entire herds hid in thorn-spiked thickets, coming out to feed only at night. Instinct told a cow to hide her calf in the grass, where its coloration made it almost invisible to wolves. When danger threatened, several cattle banded together, forming a circle around the young, their heads lowered and horns pointing outward. While a few stood guard, the rest grazed or went to drink, some relieving the guards when they were done. Like all animals, longhorns needed water. But unlike most animals, they could live on moisture from the prickly pear, a cactus they ate, thorns and all. During dry spells, longhorns wandered twenty miles in search of water, returning perhaps once a week to drink. Cold was seldom a problem in the Texas cattle country. When a norther blew, cattle showed it their backside and waited for it to pass.

The longhorn bull was one of the nastiest brutes in creation. He was so mean, in fact, that he gave daring hunters a run for their money. Hunting the wild cattle of Texas, according to a cavalry officer, was more challenging than stalking the buffalo. Buffalo fled when they caught a whiff of man-scent; longhorns charged. "To kill a buffalo," he said, "is but child's play compared to it." "If I had my choice," added another, "I should prefer a wounded bear to a wounded bull, half a dozen times over." Compared to the longhorn, the grizzly was almost "tame."[2]

Longhorns feared no man. A person afoot on the open range was a mighty fool indeed. He invited attack, and only a horse could carry him to safety—if he was fortunate. Yet even horsemen were not safe from an angry bull. The bull pawed the ground, head lowered, eyes glaring, snorting in rage. When he charged, he came like a runaway express train. If he caught his prey, horse and rider were lifted into the air, then sent crashing to earth in a tangled heap.

Bulls even went after soldiers on the march. During the Mexican War, a bull attacked American troops near Corpus Christi, Texas. Eyewitnesses compared it to a lunatic tearing into a roomful of rag dolls. He plowed into the column, scattering regiments helter-skelter, escaping before the soldiers could aim their rifles. Another time, soldiers fought a battle with a pack of wild bulls. Seeing the bulls charge, Colonel Philip Saint George Cooke ordered his men to form ranks and prepare for action. Shots were fired, several bulls killed, and several soldiers gored before the "enemy" retreated. Even so, longhorns took plenty of killing. "A bull, after receiving two [bullets] through its heart and two through its lungs, ran on a man. I have seen the heart," the colonel reported.[3]

The American settlers knew about cattle and horses and riding. Still, that knowledge, valuable as it was, meant little in Texas. They had never handled large numbers of cattle or handled them on horseback. Their Mexican neighbors, however, had been doing precisely that for three centuries. Just as they had taught the Indians to ride horses, they now taught the Texans about ranching. Vaqueros taught them how to rope cattle, round them up, brand them, and drive them long distances.

Texans even borrowed the vaquero's language. "Cow talk" was (and is) Spanish, or Spanish twisted to suit English-speakers. *Vaquero* was transformed into *buckaroo*, *rancho* into *ranch*. *Chaparreras*, leather overalls worn in thick brush, are *chaps*. *La reata* became *lariat*. *Bronco caballo*, Spanish for "rough horse," was shortened to *bronco* or *bronc*. *Rodeo* and *corral* (holding pen) are the same in both languages, although Texans pronounce them "ró-de-o" and "kr-rall." Western folk songs, like "The Streets of Laredo," are often translations of Mexican ballads.

A Mexican cowboy and his horse

Beef, not bread, was the Texans' staff of life. It was so plentiful that people ate it more often than anything else. Out on the range, they ate "jerky," a word that comes from *charquí*, Spanish for "strips of meat dried in the sun." At home, they fried steaks in melted tallow seasoned with pepper. This was hearty, stick-to-your-ribs food, guaranteed to keep you fit. Perhaps it did. An old-timer, celebrating his hundredth birthday, gave his recipe for a long life: "Live temperately in food and drinks. Try to get your beefsteaks three times a day, fried in taller. Taller is mighty healing, and there's nothing like it to keep your stumich greased-up and in good working order."[4] Back then, people believed that grease was as good for the human body as for squeaky wagon wheels. They knew nothing of the dangers of too much cholesterol and hardening of the arteries.

Melted tallow mixed with molasses also made a tasty dessert. "He sure has tallow" was Texas slang for a fat person.

Life was good in Texas, and by 1835 close to thirty-five thousand settlers were living there. Mexicans, outnumbered ten to one, came to feel like strangers in their own land. Worse, they distrusted the newcomers' intentions. Although settlers promised loyalty to Mexico, deep down they were still Americans. Indeed, some spoke openly about breaking away and bringing Texas into the Union. There was no comparison between the countries, they announced. The United States had a freely elected government. In Mexico City, General Antonio López de Santa Anna had seized power and become dictator. To control the Texans, he raised taxes and ended immigration, which only added fuel to the fire. Texans began to use explosive expressions like *tyranny* and *taxation without representation*.

Early in 1836 the settlers declared their independence and unfurled their Lone Star flag, a gold star on a blue background. Santa Anna invaded with a 6,000-man army, determined to drown the rebellion in blood. Moving swiftly, he trapped 187 Texans in the Alamo mission at San Antonio. Colonel William B. Travis, their commander, vowed to fight to the end. "I shall never surrender nor retreat," he declared. *"Victory or death."* And death it would be, beginning a cycle of hatred and reprisal that would last for generations.

General Antonio López de Santa Anna, the Mexican dictator who tried to control the Texans

The Alamo

Santa Anna had warned that he would show no mercy unless the Alamo surrendered immediately. On March 6, after a thirteen-day siege, massed Mexican army bands played the grim *degüello*—literally "the throat cutting," meaning that nobody would be taken alive when the mission fell. And that is exactly what happened. The Alamo's defenders were killed and their bodies covered with brush and burned. The "vic-

Davy Crockett *(left)* fights off Mexican attackers. He and Jim Bowie *(below)* died in the defense of the Alamo.

Sam Houston,
commander of the Texan army

tory" cost Santa Anna 1,550 men—8 attackers for each defender.

The dictator grew bolder. Two weeks later, at Goliad, he had 350 Texans shot after promising them mercy if they surrendered. Then, on April 23, the tide turned. On that day General Sam Houston, commander of the Texas army, surprised him at the San Jacinto River. It was the Mexicans' afternoon siesta, and Houston's men gave them a rude awakening. Shouting "Remember the Alamo!" they broke through a line of sleepy sentries and tore into the camp with rifles and bowie knives. Their vengeance was awful. In just eighteen minutes, 630 Mexicans were killed; 9 Texans died and 26 were wounded. Bodies of men and horses lay in heaps, attracting coyotes. In time the bodies dried up and cows chewed the bones, spoiling their milk until farmers buried the remains. There were also 730 prisoners taken, including Santa Anna. Threatened with bowie knives, he agreed to remove his army and recognize Texan independence. Soon after returning to Mexico, he fell from power.

The new Mexican government refused to go along with the deal. Santa Anna's promises, they insisted, had been made under the threat of death and were therefore meaningless. Texas was not independent. Mexican troops could go wherever they wished in Mexican territory. During the next nine years, they launched repeated raids into the Lone Star Republic. Mexican forces twice captured San Antonio, only to be driven off with losses on both sides. Matters came to a head in December 1845, after Texas joined the Union as the twenty-eighth state. Mexico refused to accept the Rio Grande as an international boundary and, after several border clashes, the United States Congress declared war.

The Mexican War (1846–1848) was the nation's first war on foreign soil, and many opposed it angrily. People like Abraham Lincoln called it a war of aggression, a bully's war and a disgrace

Santa Anna as a prisoner. After his defeat at the battle of San Jacinto, the Mexican leader was forced to recognize the independence of Texas.

An old print shows an American soldier during the Mexican War.

to the United States. Ulysses S. Grant agreed with his future commander in chief. Although Grant served as a junior officer, he found the war "one of the most unjust ever waged by a stronger against a weaker nation."[5]

Mexico was no match for its neighbor. American forces lost no time in occupying California and New Mexico. Meantime, the main army invaded Mexico proper, defeated its army, and captured its capital city. It was a war that did little credit to either side. Mexicans shot prisoners. Americans shot prisoners—and did much more. General Winfield Scott, the American field commander, denounced his own troops. They had, he said, committed atrocities like murder, robbery, and rape all along the Rio Grande.

The peace treaty was seen by Mexicans as another kind of atrocity. It forced them to accept the Rio Grande as the border and give up California, New Mexico, and Arizona. But the big surprise was yet to come. As if to add insult to injury, gold was found in California nine days before the treaty signing. Since communications were slow, the signers knew nothing of the discovery. No wonder Mexicans felt cheated. To this day they have a saying: Poor Mexico! So far from God and so close to the United States.

General Winfield Scott led American forces in the capture of Mexico City. He later became general-in-chief of the U.S. Army.

The two peoples remained bitter enemies. Mexicans spoke with contempt of everyone north of the Rio Grande. They were, they said mockingly, *gringos*, from "Green Grow the Lilacs," the invaders' favorite song. Westerners, particularly Texans, had all sorts of names for Mexicans—mostly insulting. Mexicans were regarded as racially inferior, people who deserved no respect or consideration. According to one Texan, a lawman no less: "I can maintain a better stomach at the killing of a Mexican than at the crushing of a body louse."[6]

Border raids continued. Although raiders crossed from both sides of the Rio Grande, the Texans were more aggressive by far. From the time of the Alamo to the end of the Mexican War, they targeted Mexican-owned ranches in Texas. The raiders were often wild, undisciplined youths. Respectable people called them cowboys.

The term did not originate in Texas. As near as we can tell, *cowboy* appeared during the American Revolution. Then, and for nearly a century thereafter, it was no compliment. Normally, it was a fighting word, an insult. The term was first used in Westchester County, New York, to refer to Tories, colonial traitors who fired from ambush. Cowboys hid in thick brush, tinkled a cowbell to lure a patriot farmer looking for a lost cow, and shot him without warning. Patriots killed cowboys on sight. Only after the Civil War was the term applied to a hired man who worked with cattle for a living.

The favorite hunting ground of the early Texas cowboys lay between the Nueces and the Rio Grande rivers. On moonlit nights, fifteen or twenty cowboys would make off with hundreds of head of cattle from ranches owned by Mexicans, selling them as far away as Louisiana. The Mexican ranchers themselves had no market value. Those not killed outright were so scared that they abandoned their property and fled for their lives. By 1850, Texans had taken over everything the Mexicans had left behind. From then on, thanks to the cowboys, ranching was almost entirely an American business.

The Mexicans did not accept defeat meekly. Although their lands were gone, they struck back whenever they had the opportunity. *Banditos* continued to raid Texas to "collect grandfather's cattle," as they called it, and the Texans answered in kind. Across-the-border raids continued into the early years of the twentieth century. The last raid occurred in 1916, when Pancho Villa attacked Columbus, New Mexico, killing sixteen people and burning much of the town. Even so, these raids were tame compared to the Comanche troubles.

As Texas grew, pioneers pushed west and northwest of the original settlements. By the 1840s they reached the Great Plains, where they met the Comanche. It was a meeting of fire and gunpowder.

The Comanche saw the Texans as invaders, like the Spaniards before them, out to steal their hunting grounds. These, they believed, were gifts of the Great Spirit to be defended with their lives. The Texans, however, saw things differently. Having defeated Mexico, they felt entitled to enjoy their prize. They had more right to the land than a pack of what they saw as "heathen redskins." No one can be sure who struck the first blow. All we know is that it was struck, and the cruelty and killing that followed became ingrained in both peoples. The result was a fight to the finish. Only one people could rule the southern plains. The other would be broken completely and forever.

It was by no means certain that the Texans would win. The Comanche were magnificent warriors. They had resisted the Mexicans for over a century and had lost none of their fighting spirit. On summer nights, groups of horsemen set out from distant camps. They rode single file, forming a thin, almost invisible, line on the moonlit plains. Avoiding strongly defended places, they struck easy targets like travelers and isolated farm families. Whites, taken by surprise, could not defend themselves. Frequently, their first warning of danger was the last thing they ever saw or heard. Usually it came in the hours before dawn, the time of deepest sleep. There would be a war whoop, the sound of axes smashing a cabin door, and screams of pain.

The first brave to touch a fallen victim gave a shout of victory. "*A-he! A-he!*"—"I claim it!" What he claimed was the victim's scalp. Scalping was an ancient custom in North America; warrior tribes, east and west, took scalps. Scalps were not merely war trophies. Indians had noticed that hair is almost the only part of the human body that continues to grow through an entire

Little Spaniard by George Catlin
(National Museum of American Art, Washington/Art Resource, New York)

Buffalo Chase, Mouth of the Yellowstone by George Catlin
(National Museum of American Art, Washington/Art Resource, New York)

lifetime. It grew, they believed, because it contained the person's spirit, and therefore had magical power. Scalping was a way of capturing the spirit and preventing it from taking revenge.

Once a victim went down, the brave grabbed his (or her) hair with one hand and cut a circle around the scalp with a knife. A quick jerk brought it away from the skull. The scalp was then dried on a frame and hung on the warrior's belt or on a pole outside his tepee. Although all victims were scalped, Indians preferred white men.

Indians usually have very little hair on their bodies; white men can have beards, hairy chests, and hairy underarms. This body hair was taken and woven into strands for decorating buckskin shirts, leggings, and weapons. In addition, a victim's fingers might be cut off, dried, and strung on necklaces.

The dead got off easy; they were beyond pain. Captives suffered dreadfully until released by death. Adult male prisoners were always tortured. The Comanche knew a great deal about

This painting by Frederic Remington depicts Comanche warriors surrounding a wagon train guarded by soldiers.

A woman settler tries to prevent an Indian from entering.

human anatomy, where to cause the most suffering while keeping the victim alive as long as possible. Captives were spared nothing. They were cut, stabbed, burned, scratched, scraped, torn, beaten, and their bones broken. The soles of their feet might be sliced off and the victim forced to walk on the tender stumps.

Women and children fared little better. As we have seen, Indians kidnapped them in order to marry, enslave, or adopt them into their tribes. Texas women were no exception. Newspapers and diaries of the time are full of stories like that of Matilda Lochkart. When Matilda, a pretty sixteen-year-old, was taken in 1840, she aroused her kidnappers' sense of "humor." Each morning as she lay sleeping, they touched her with a coal from the campfire, then roared with laughter at her screams.

Returned when her people paid ransom, they could hardly recognize her when she arrived in San Antonio. A friend wrote in her diary: "Her head, arms and face were full of bruises, and sores, and her nose was actually burnt off to the bone—all but the fleshy end gone, and a great scab formed on the end of the bone. Both nostrils were wide open and denuded of flesh. She told a piteous tale of how dreadfully the Indians had beaten her, and how they would wake her from sleep by sticking a chunk of fire to her flesh, especially to her nose . . . her body had many scars from the fire."[7]

In October 1835 the Texas government formed special units described as "ranging companies." At first, these consisted of local people who served in time of danger, like a volunteer fire department today. But the need was so great that the volunteers soon became a full-time force—the Texas Rangers. Rangers "ranged"; that is, they were constantly on the move. Their duty was to guard the border with Mexico, patrol the countryside, and carry the fight to the enemy to keep him off balance. This required men of unusual ability. By definition, the Texas Ranger was brave; courage was taken for granted and never discussed. A coward could not have lasted a day. To do his job, and live to tell about it, the Texas Ranger had to be four men rolled into one. According to the saying: A Texas Ranger can ride like a Mexican, trail like an Indian, shoot like a Tennessean, and fight like a very devil. Nevertheless, these traits were not enough.

Americans had never fought mounted Indians until the 1830s. They had no experience with this kind of warfare and were always at a disadvantage. The problem was one of weapons. Indian weapons were ideal for a fast-paced battle on horseback. To protect himself, the brave carried a shield of buffalo hide so tough that a bullet would bounce off harmlessly, unless it struck head-on. For attack, he used a fourteen-foot lance and a bow and arrows tipped with bone or flint; traders later sold him sheet metal for making arrowheads. He carried up to a hundred arrows and could shoot these from a galloping horse. It was not unusual for a brave to shoot twenty arrows and ride three hundred yards in a minute. An arrow hit with such force that it could tear through the body of a buffalo—or a person—pop out the other side, and keep going.

When the Texans came onto the plains, they still had the weapons of the forest. These were fine weapons but of little value there. The pistol fired a lead ball that could shatter a man's skull at twenty yards. The long rifle was even deadlier. Unfortunately, these guns held only one bullet at a time, and were heavy and slow to reload; a trained soldier could fire only two shots a minute. This is why the first Texas Rangers *never* charged Comanche on horseback. They dismounted, left a guard with the horses, and fought on foot. But unless they killed a few braves quickly, frightening the others away, they were in big trouble. A brave could shoot ten arrows in the time it took a Texas Ranger to fire one shot and reload. The Comanche came like a whirlwind, shouting and shooting. If they rode in among men with empty guns, they ran them through with their lances.

The Texans needed a hard-hitting weapon that could fire faster and farther than an Indian could shoot his arrows. It would have to be both lightweight and powerful, easy to use on horseback, and fire several times without reloading. They needed Samuel Colt's revolver.

Born in Connecticut in 1814, Samuel Colt was fascinated by guns from an early age. He became a sailor and, upon turning sixteen, shipped out for India. During the long voyage, he had plenty of time to think about his favorite subject. One day he went up to the wheelhouse, from where the helmsman steered the vessel. He had been there often, but that day was special. For the first time he saw—really saw—the steering wheel. It was round, with handgrips radiating from a central hub. He realized that this arrangement was ideal for guns.

Using his pocketknife, Colt carved a wooden model of a pistol. It had six chambers, each holding one bullet, set in a cylinder that revolved behind a gun barrel. To shoot the pistol, you drew back the hammer, or firing pin, and squeezed the trigger. After each shot the hammer was drawn back again, turning the cylinder and bringing another chamber into line with the barrel. When the pistol was empty, you opened the cylinder and loaded a fresh bullet into each chamber. Colt's "revolver" was actually six pistols in one, truly a "six-gun," or "six-shooter." Returning home, he patented his invention and built a factory in Paterson, New Jersey. Later, the repeating rifle was invented, an accurate long-range

Colt six-shooters, as they appear in a Sears Roebuck catalog of 1897

weapon. But Colt's revolver was the gun that won the West.

No one knows how the six-shooter first came to Texas, but it soon became *the* weapon of the Texas Rangers. It proved itself on June 8, 1844, at the Battle of the Padernales River. Fifteen Texas Rangers had set out from San Antonio after a Comanche war party. But instead of a small party, as expected, they found seventy-five braves. Actually, the Comanche found them. They came from behind, taking them by surprise. Normally, the rangers would have tried to outrun the Comanche or take cover behind rocks—if rocks were nearby. But not this time. The Rangers turned and charged.

"Powder-burn them!" shouted Captain Jack Hays, their commander, as he spurred his mount. Hays led his men into the midst of the Comanche, bolts of fire striking from their fists as they came. The Indians were stunned at the fury of the attack. Never before had Texas Rangers fought them on horseback. And never before had so many braves been shot out of the saddle in so short a time. Their wounds were horrible. Six-shooters fired at close range not only tore gaping holes in flesh but set clothing on fire. Now it was the Comanche who turned tail, leaving a trail of discarded shields, bows, and lances. Although two or three rangers died, thirty braves bit the dust. The Comanche had learned a lesson. "I will never again fight Jack Hays, who has a shot for every finger of the hand," said their chief.

That day on the Padernales marked a turning point. The Comanche were still dangerous and would remain so for another thirty years. But they were no longer a mortal danger. The Texas Rangers and Sam Colt's six-gun allowed the white man to fight the Plains Indians on horseback. The whites had come out onto the Great Plains to stay.

Talk of a "cattle kingdom" would have seemed strange in the 1840s. True, Texans had plenty of cattle, but that was hardly a comfort. Cattle were so plentiful as to be nearly worthless. The only market for them was the local "hide and tallow" factories located along the Gulf of Mexico. There the animals were butchered. The factories took whatever they needed, and the rest was left to the buzzards. Apart from this, however, there was little demand for longhorns.

Not that Americans in the East did not want beef. They did, very much, only there was no easy way of getting it from Texas. The closest market was over a thousand miles from the Lone Star State. Railroads were being built back East, but these were still far away. It would take a generation for them to reach the Great Plains.

Nevertheless, some ranchers did try to walk their cattle to other markets. The discovery of gold brought a flood of prospectors, or forty-niners, to California. So many came that even the native herds could not satisfy the demand for beef. Prices skyrocketed, reaching $125 a head, an outlandish price; even scrawny calves brought $25. To Texans, cattle-rich and money-poor, that was real money. During the 1850s, several herds were driven to the goldfields around San Francisco. It was a long journey, filled with danger and hardship. More than one Texan wound up with his scalp dangling from an Apache belt. Herds crossed stretches of desert, leaving behind dead cattle to become mounds of bleached bones. You could see them for miles, glittering snow-white in the sun. If, after a year, the beef made it to the goldfields, the cowboys cashed in—big. They had also set records for endurance, but it was not something they wanted to repeat. Few did.

Another market was New Orleans, at the mouth of the Mississippi River. Instead of crossing deserts, herds had to pass through swamps. Abel "Shanghai" Pierce, a well-known Texas rancher, made the trip once. It was a slippery journey, but Shanghai treated it as a joke to show how smart longhorns could be. Whenever they came to quicksand, he said, winking, they hooked their horns onto wild grapevines and swung across like monkeys. That so amused his horse that it laughed out loud!

New York City saw its first longhorns in 1854. Two cowmen, Thomas Candy Pointing and Washington Malone, drove seven hundred head to Muncie, Indiana, where they put them aboard a train with stockcars. The animals were unloaded in upper Manhattan and herded downtown, along Third Avenue, to a market at Twenty-fourth Street. New Yorkers, like all city people at that time, were used to seeing all sorts of animals—cattle, horses, hogs, sheep, goats—driven through their streets. But longhorns were different. They stampeded, overflowing the side-

walks and clearing them of pedestrians. Panic swept Third Avenue as mothers grabbed youngsters and pulled them indoors. Grown men ran for their lives, a few slipping in the muddy, manure-filled gutters. The longhorns had "something of a wild look," the *Daily Tribune* noted, adding that their meat was "a little tough cooked in the ordinary way." Nevertheless, they brought eighty dollars a head.

There is no telling what would have happened had this long-distance trade continued. But that was not to be. In 1861, eleven Southern states seceded from the Union, forming a separate nation and triggering the Civil War. Texas became part of the new nation, the Confederate States of America.

The Civil War affected all Texans. Most able-bodied men joined the rebel armies and saw action in scores of battles. Those who remained behind showed their patriotism in various ways. Among them were cowboys, who by now were becoming

A cattle drive in Louisiana. The herds had to pass through swamps on the way to New Orleans.

General Ulysses S. Grant attacking Vicksburg, Mississippi, in July 1863. The fall of Vicksburg split the Confederacy.

respectable. Cowboys helped the Texas Rangers patrol the Mexican border and fight the Comanche. They also delivered cattle to the Confederate armies. That took "more guts than you can hang on a fence"[8]—true courage—if they had to swim a herd across the Mississippi. Men and animals drowned, but the gray-clad soldiers got their beef. At least they did until July 1863, when General Ulysses S. Grant took Vicksburg, Mississippi, gaining control of the river and splitting the Confederacy in half.

Meantime, with their men away, ranch families moved to town, leaving their cattle to care for themselves. Families made do with basic food: beef, bacon, sweet potatoes, vegetables. But most other items were in short supply, thanks to the Union blockade. Women solved the clothing shortage by spinning cotton and weaving it into cloth. "Coffee" was made from ground acorns or, said one joker, "with anything that turned brown in a dirty pot." Soap was made by filling a barrel with wood ashes and pouring in water at the top. The water soaked the ashes, took the lye out of them, and leaked through holes at the bottom of the barrel. Lye-water was then mixed with tallow and molded into cakes of soap.

The soldiers returned after the Confederate surrender in April 1865. It was a grim homecoming. Many were wounded, and all were exhausted after years at the front. Abandoned ranches needed repairs, which cost money. Texans had plenty of worthless Confederate money. What they needed were Yankee dollars, "Lincoln skins," as they called them with a sneer.

Except for cattle, they had nothing to sell. The herds had multiplied in their absence. At least four million branded cattle and mavericks—(pronounced "*mav*-ricks"), unbranded animals belonging to no one—roamed the range. Unfortunately, markets were still far away, making cattle only slightly more valuable than Confederate money. A traveling peddler, for example, would trade an ordinary clock for four cows; along his route he might collect four hundred longhorns from people without money. Families traded cattle in Mexico, where twenty full-grown longhorns brought a sack of coffee, two sets of knives and forks, and two pairs of spurs.

Still, there was hope. That fall, copies of the *New York Daily Tribune* brought exciting news. The folks up north wanted beef. During the war, the government had combed the country for cattle to feed the Union armies. So many were butchered that production fell, causing prices to rise. In New York City, for instance, sirloin steaks went for twenty-five cents a pound. That is cheap nowadays, but it was a small fortune back then. Prices were so high that factory workers could not afford to put beef on the table.

Suddenly those millions of longhorns became a treasure on the hoof. Cattle were worth no more than $4 a head on the open range. But those same animals could bring $40 up north. If one could assemble a small herd, say a thousand head worth $4,000, it would bring $40,000, for a profit of $36,000, less expenses. That was more money than prewar cattlemen could have earned in a lifetime. But how to get those $4 cows to the $40 market?

The answer was the iron horse. Railroad construction had slowed during the Civil War, but once the fighting ended, Congress encouraged building with offers of money and land to the railroad companies. The goal was a transcontinental railroad to join the Atlantic and Pacific coasts, binding the nation with belts of steel. Gandy dancers, gangs of Irish immigrants, began laying track westward from the Missouri River, while gangs of Chinese coolies pushed eastward across the Rockies from Cal-

Railroad construction picked up after the Civil War. This lithograph by Currier and Ives depicts the railroad on the plains.

ifornia. By the spring of 1866, the rails would reach Sedalia, Missouri. Sedalia, of course, was nowhere near Texas, but still a lot closer than Chicago and New York. From there cattle could be shipped cheaply to the great industrial cities.

Texans set to work. Each day they rode onto the range in search of their strayed cattle and to brand any maverick they could put a rope on. By early spring, they were ready. As the plains turned green with new grass, 260,000 cattle, representing dozens of herds, began to stream northward. They went up the Shawnee Trail through Dallas, crossed the Red River into Indian Territory (the future state of Oklahoma), and entered southeastern Kansas near Baxter Springs. And that is where their troubles began.

Since before the Civil War, longhorns were known to bring the dreaded Texas fever. Although immune to it themselves, they carried the ticks that carried the virus that caused the disease. Wherever they passed, farm cattle sickened and died. To protect their own livestock, Kansas and Missouri had passed quarantine laws against driving longhorns in the warm months, when the ticks were active. In effect, that ended all drives, since no one in his right mind would move cattle across the plains in winter.

The year 1866 brought out farmers with shotguns, determined to keep the longhorns away from their property. Worse, it brought out bands of thieves called jayhawkers. Using the law as an excuse, they demanded money to allow the Texans to pass. Those who refused to pay, or could not pay, were turned back or had their herds stampeded at night. Several herds were wiped out, shot down to the last animal.

One day Jim Daugherty, a lad of sixteen with his own herd, ran into some jayhawkers. Without uttering a word, they killed one of his cowboys and took him prisoner. Daugherty was tied to a tree and whipped until he promised to return to Texas. He agreed but continued north as soon as he was set free. Instead of heading for Sedalia, though, he drove his cattle westward, swung northward around Kansas, and finally sold his cattle in Iowa.

Those who followed Daugherty's lead were seldom as fortunate. It was an ordeal, as cattleman George Duffield complained in his diary:

This engraving of Jim Daugherty being whipped by jayhawkers shows him as a grown man, not as a boy of sixteen.

Upset our wagon in River & lost Many of our cooking utencils . . . was on my Horse the whole night & it raining hard . . . Lost my knife. . . . There was one of our party Drowned to day (Mr. Carr) & Several narrow escapes & I among [them]. . . . Many Men in trouble. Horses *all* give out & Men refused to do anything. . . . Awful night . . . not having had a bite to eat for 60 hours . . . *Tired.* . . . Indians very troublesome. . . . Oh! what a night— Thunder Lightning & rain—we followed our Beeves *all* night as they wandered about. . . . We Hauled cattle out of the Mud with oxen half the day. . . . Dark days are these for me. Nothing but Bread & Coffee. Hands all Growling & Swearing—every thing wet & cold . . . Sick & discouraged. Have *not* got the *Blues* but I am in *Hel of a fix.* . . . My back is Blistered bad. . . . Indians saucy . . . one man down with Boils and one with Ague [fever]. . . . Found a Human skeleton on the Prairie to day.[9]

Most of the herds waited at Baxter Springs, Kansas, to see what would happen. Unable to go forward, herds piled up south of the town and remained there all summer. By fall, the grass was nearly gone, helped along by farmers who set prairie fires. The Texans, desperate for money, took any offer, often written on a bad check. The unsold cattle froze during the winter. In the end, only a tiny fraction of the cattle that had left Texas the year before benefited their owners.

Nevertheless, the Texans had no choice but to try again next season. That was not something they looked forward to with confidence. There was too much danger, too much uncertainty, in the cattle business. What they needed was a market near a railroad, beyond the reach of jayhawkers and farmers.

Joseph G. McCoy had the answers. Born in Illinois in 1837, McCoy began his career as a livestock dealer before the Civil War. A big, husky fellow with a booming voice, he had grand ideas about cattle, railroads, and money. The three went together. His aim was to attract herds to a central point along a railroad line, where owners and dealers could meet and do business. The success of that idea made him the original "real McCoy." His nickname was well deserved, for while others raised cattle, he created the largest cattle market in history.

Joseph G. McCoy turned Abilene, Kansas, into a center of the cattle industry. Abilene was the first cow town.

Not that he created it single-handedly. By the spring of 1867, the gandy dancers had reached eastern Kansas. Each day, their rails stretched farther and farther across the plains. At the same time, Kansas changed its quarantine law to allow Texas cattle to be driven west of the settled farm areas. That was all McCoy needed to know. It was the chance of a lifetime, and he grabbed it with both hands.

McCoy persuaded the Kansas Pacific Railroad to ship cattle at special rates from Kansas to Chicago, Illinois, capital of the meat-packing industry. After a careful search, he chose a place called Abilene for his market. The name, which its first residents took from the Bible, means "city of the plains." Calling it a city, however, was like calling a tomcat a tiger. "Abilene in 1867," McCoy recalled, "was a very small, dead place, consisting of about one dozen log huts, low, small rude affairs, four-fifths of which were covered with dirt for roofing. . . . The business of the burg was conducted in two small rooms, mere log huts, and of course the inevitable saloon, also in a log hut,

A street in Abilene, Kansas, about the year 1870. The street was unpaved, and the sidewalk made of wooden boards.

was also to be found." Its only "export" was prairie dogs, sold as souvenirs to tourists at five dollars a pair. For a city person, it stood at the far end of nowhere. For a cattleman, it was the promised land. Abilene was nothing less than an island set in a sea of grass, ideal for holding cattle awaiting sale.

McCoy went to work. Land next to the village was purchased for shipping yards. Lumber was brought in by train, along with carpenters to build holding pens, loading chutes, an office, a barn, and a three-story hotel. For a while that hotel, the Drovers' Cottage, was the unofficial headquarters of the American cattle industry. During the trail-driving season, guests sat on the porch and "talked cow." Millions of dollars changed hands in the dining room each week. Few contracts were signed on the dotted line; men simply shook hands and the deal was done.

McCoy sent a scout toward the Shawnee Trail to spread the word about Abilene. Texans, however, were suspicious. Having been hurt so badly the year before, Abilene seemed too good to be true. Reluctantly, yet hoping against hope, they turned their herds northward. They were not disappointed. All of the thirty-five thousand longhorns that reached Abilene were sold and shipped east. It was a good start, but nothing compared to what followed.

McCoy prepared for the 1868 season in a big way. To attract eastern buyers, he organized the first Wild West show. Seven Texas cowboys and Mexican vaqueros were hired to catch the largest buffalo they could find. Three of these, including a magnificent twenty-three-hundred-pound bull, were loaded into a reinforced railroad car and sent to Chicago. Draped on each side of the car was a banner reading ABILENE, KANSAS, THE MARKET FOR TEXAS CATTLE. Whenever the train stopped along the way, people flocked to see the show. There had never been anything like it before. They gaped at the shaggy, red-eyed buffalo. They thrilled at the Texans' roping skills and the Mexicans' riding tricks. Newspapers carried full reports, illustrated with drawings of daring deeds. Buyers flocked to Abilene.

A picture from Joseph G. McCoy's 1874 book, *Historical Sketches of the Cattle Trade*. A shrewd businessman, McCoy hired cowboys to capture buffalo bulls, which were put on display in Chicago to encourage cattle buyers to come to Abilene.

John Simpson Chisum, one of Texas's most prosperous ranchers, furnished cattle to the Confederate army during the Civil War.

Meantime, McCoy sent scouts to meet the herds coming up from Texas. Cattlemen, they said, needn't bother with the Sedalia Trail anymore. There was another trail, a better trail, closer to the railroad, named for Jesse Chisholm (pronounced "*Chizum*"), the son of a Scottish father and a Cherokee mother. Chisholm was a trader who had bargained with the Indians for furs and buffalo robes. At the close of the Civil War, he hauled goods by wagon from his camp on the Arkansas River in Kansas to the Washita River in Indian Territory, marking the way with mounds of earth. McCoy's scouts extended the trail south to the Red River and north to Abilene. Chisholm himself never saw Abilene; he died after eating spoiled bear grease just as McCoy first set eyes on the place. But the Chisholm Trail quickly became a legend among cattlemen. For generations, "The Old Chisholm Trail" was a favorite cowboy song. Men gathered around campfires to sing:

> Come along, boys, and listen to my tale,
> I'll tell you of my troubles on the old Chisholm Trail.
>
> Coma ti ti youpy, youpy yea, youpy yea,
> Coma ti ti youpy, youpy yea.
>
> I woke up one morning on the old Chisholm Trail,
> Rope in my hand and a cow by the tail.
>
> Coma ti ti, etc.
>
> Feet in the stirrups, seat in the saddle,
> I hung and rattled with them longhorn cattle.
>
> Coma ti ti, etc.

Herds crowded the Chisholm Trail, bound for Abilene. About 75,000 longhorns arrived there in 1868; 350,000 in 1869; 300,000 in 1870; and 700,000 in 1871. Then the bottom dropped out. As settlers moved westward, starting farms and villages, Kansas lawmakers pushed the quarantine line farther west. Abilene had to give up the cattle trade at the end of the 1871 season.

Other Kansas towns, beyond the line, welcomed the cattlemen

The Arizona Cowboy by Frederic S. Remington
(The Rockwell Museum, Corning, New York; photo by Charles Swain)

Cowboys from the Bar Triangle by Charles M. Russell
(Buffalo Bill Historical Center, Cody, Wyoming; gift of William E. Weiss)

The early days of the Chisholm Trail. Having gotten the herd into a long line, the cowboys try to keep it moving at a slow, steady pace. Rushing things along caused the cattle to lose weight, which was the same as losing money for their owners.

with open arms. Newton in 1871; Ellsworth, 1871 to 1875; Wichita, 1872 to 1876: Each had its day as a cow town until overtaken by the quarantine. Finally there was Dodge City on the Atchison, Topeka and Santa Fe Railroad. Dodge held the record. For eight years, 1877 to 1885, she was "queen of the cow towns." The Chisholm Trail had been abandoned by then. Grass covered the ruts, erasing any sign of it. A new trail, the Western Trail, passed through Dodge and continued on to Fort Buford, North Dakota. But nothing could stop the advance of the quarantine line, and Dodge's best days ended in 1885. From then on, Texas cattle were forbidden to enter Kansas. An era had ended.

The years 1866 to 1885 saw the rise and fall of trail driving. In that time, more than eight million longhorns came up the trails from Texas. By then, however, ranches stretched across all of the Great Plains. In just one generation, the cattle kingdom spread from Texas to Oklahoma, Kansas, Nebraska, the Dakotas, Montana, Wyoming, Nevada, Utah, Colorado, Arizona, and New Mexico. At its height, this cattle kingdom covered an area of 130 million acres. It changed a nation's eating habits. Never before, in the entire span of human history, were so many people able to have meat on a regular basis.

None of this could have happened without the cowboy. The way he lived—or the way people *thought* he lived—has become part of our American heritage.

CHAPTER THREE
The Man on Horseback

"There *is* something romantic about him. He
lives on horseback, as do the Bedouins; he fights
on horseback, as did the knights of chivalry; he
goes armed with a strange new weapon which he
uses ambidextrously and precisely; he swears
like a trooper, drinks like a fish, wears clothes
like an actor, and fights like a devil. He is
gracious to ladies, reserved toward strangers,
generous to his friends, and brutal to his
enemies. He is a cowboy, a typical Westerner."

—Walter Prescott Webb, *The Great Plains*

WE KNOW A GREAT DEAL ABOUT THE AMERICAN COWBOY.
Several wrote autobiographies, which make fascinating reading.
Charles A. Siringo's *Texas Cow Boy; or, Fifteen Years on the
Hurricane Deck of a Spanish Pony*, Andy Adams's *Log of a
Cowboy*, and Teddy Blue Abbott's *We Pointed Them North*
are classics. In addition, there are files of frontier newspapers,
collections of photographs, and the "oral tradition": songs, stories, poetry, and slang. Last, but not least, are paintings by
artists who saw the old-time cowboy in action. Among the best
are the works of Frederic Remington and Charles M. Russell,
himself a working cowboy. Their paintings may be seen in art
museums across the country. The leading collections of western

Black cowboys in Texas, about 1890. A large proportion of cowboys were former slaves and sons of slaves, who sought opportunity in the West after the Civil War.

art are in the Amon Carter Museum, Fort Worth, Texas, and the Thomas Gilcrease Institute, Tulsa, Oklahoma.

An estimated thirty-five thousand men drove cattle up the trails from Texas between 1866 and 1885. Cattle driving was strenuous work, young man's work, and cowboys ranged in age from the midteens to the early thirties; the average age was twenty-four. "Old hands" were in their forties, but there were very few of these. Your typical cowboy was a Texan by birth or a southerner who had gone there after the Civil War, a bold, brash bundle of energy who carried himself with confidence. He rode into town waving his hat, firing his six-gun into the air, and yelling to wake the dead. *"Yip-Yip-Yip-e-e-e-e-e-e-e! Yah-ah-ah-Yah-e-e-e-e-e-e-e!"* He called it the cowboy yell. Yankees had known it as the rebel yell.

Not all cowboys, however, were former rebels. About one in ten was a Mexican who either lived in Texas or traveled back and forth across the border seeking work. Mexicans were outnumbered by blacks, freed slaves from East Texas cotton plantations and men who had come west for a fresh start in life.

They easily fit into the world of the frontier; there was plenty to do, and employers didn't care about race or background if they got an honest day's work. Blacks took jobs as stagecoach drivers, teamsters, mule skinners, and railroad men. Those who became cowboys worked as ropers, trail hands, broncobusters, and cooks; about one in five cowboys was a former slave or the son of a slave. Former slaves and former rebels, who had fought to keep slavery, now found themselves working together as freemen. We get an idea of what this meant from books such as *The Life and Adventures of Nat Love by Himself*, the story of a black cowboy who saw the West at its wildest and woolliest.

During the heyday of the open range, blacks lived better there than anywhere else in the United States. Still, old prejudices lingered. Blacks might be respected as individuals but not as a people. Only one black on record became a trail boss, the man in charge of a herd. His name was Al Jones. In town, blacks were generally not allowed to sit near whites in restaurants. Anyone with other ideas might be beaten up and tossed headfirst into the street. One fellow was branded on the thigh with a red-hot shovel for speaking his mind about rebels. A few blacks became ranchers, owning small "spreads" of their own. Among them was 80 John Wallace, an ex-slave who saved enough money to buy a ranch and stock it with six hundred head of cattle.

Apart from their skin color, cowboys were pretty much alike. They might, of course, be tall or short, but they had the same body type. Look at any group picture and try to find a fat cowboy. You will not. Cowboys were thin, wiry men, which explains why Slim was such a popular nickname. That made a lot of sense, for the thinner the man, the easier it was for a horse to carry him long distances. Fat men were hard on horses, tiring them quickly.

The cowboy was a proud man. According to Teddy Blue, "while cowpunchers were common men without education, they set themselves away above people who chances are were no more common or uneducated than themselves." Pride had nothing to do with income, although, as we shall see, the cowboy was paid better than most city workers. It came from skill and a way of life. Only a cowboy rode horses, handled longhorns,

Nat Love wrote his biography, which tells of the life of a black cowboy in the Old West.

and wore a six-gun during a normal day's work. It was assumed that he knew his job and would always do his best. He did not like to be ordered around. At the first blunt word from his boss, he'd tell him what to do with the job and pack his gear. There was always another job elsewhere, no questions asked.

Cowboys made their own rules suited to their special needs. These rules were not written down, but everyone knew them and was expected to obey without hesitation. They were the westerner's version of the golden rule: Do unto others as you would have them do unto you. That made sense on the frontier. No one, however strong or clever, could survive alone out there; everyone depended upon everyone else. Helping someone in need was a kind of insurance policy, because someday you might be in the same boat.

Helping took different forms. If a cowboy fell ill, another filled in without being asked or expecting to be thanked. If the cook needed water, the first man into camp fetched it. Above all, there was loyalty and courage. In this, the cowboy was like the soldier or the Texas Ranger. Loyalty meant that he put the welfare of the group above his own personal interests. In his case the group, or outfit, or bunch, handled longhorns. That was dangerous work, and he literally trusted his comrades with his life. You had to know that your sidekick had "gravel in the gizzard," that he would support you, come what may. But there was no trusting a coward. He was, in western slang, "as yeller as mustard without the bite." He was a "booger," someone who scared easily.

Honesty was another rule in cattle country. The picture of the West as a rootin'-tootin' wilderness of blazing six-shooters is exaggerated. There was dishonesty, to be sure, but on the whole, people trusted each other. You assumed that others were honest, and usually they were.

Nobody bothered to lock up; indeed, few places had locks at all. A lock meant you doubted people's honesty. Doan's Store, just south of the Red River on the Chisholm Trail, was typical. At the end of a day, the owners shut the door and went home. But that did not mean the store was "closed." Any passing cowboy, without a place to sleep, could let himself in for the night and stretch out on a counter or on the floor. If he needed

A Remington sketch of a typical cowboy

anything, he took it, leaving money to pay for it. If he was broke, he went off with the goods without paying. Yet the owners never lost a penny during their twenty years in business. Sooner or later, the cowboy sent the money or rode hundreds of miles to pay up in person. It was a matter of personal honor.

The same rule applied to private homes and trail camps. Since people expected visitors to be honest, they were always welcome. Hospitality was freely offered. If, for example, a family went to town, it simply shut the front door and left. No one gave a thought to burglars or to leaving a guard behind. Some families even left notes for would-be callers: "Make yourself at home, and feed the chickens when you go." Likewise, a hungry stranger, coming upon a trail camp, did not wait for an invitation to dinner. If the cowboys were there, he sat down with them; if not, he cooked and ate whatever he wanted. No payment was asked or offered, since that was an insult. "Every ranch, in fact even every dugout," an easterner wrote, "was a free inn for the hungry and weary, and a generous welcome greeted the new-comer at the door."[1]

Hospitality, however, did not mean familiarity. When among cowboys, you kept your hands to yourself, unless you meant to fight. You never slapped a cowboy on the back, even if he was your oldest friend. Nor did you expect him to talk about himself. A man's private life, or past life, was no one's business but his own. You could work next to a fellow for years without learning his real name. He was always Snake-Head, Itchy Jake, Six-gun Bob, Curley, Tex, Never Slip, or a thousand other nicknames. He might volunteer more information, but if he didn't, you would not ask. That was "hornin' in," meddling in others' affairs. Meddlers were put in their place with a few sharp words. They were told that they suffered from "diarrhea of the jawbone," or that "the bigger the mouth the better it looks when shut."

The cowboy's language was vivid and earthy, like the man himself. He shaped his words to suit his needs and had many ways of saying the same thing. *To go*, for example, was a common action. You could be "on the go" for various reasons, in various ways, and at various speeds. If you were not in a hurry, you "ambled," "jogged," or "moseyed along." But if the Comanche were coming, or the herd stampeded, you would "git," "va-

"hornin' in"

"moseyed along"

"vamoose"

➤➤➤ **61**

moose," "light out," "burn the earth," "hit the breeze," and "rattle your hocks." If safety wasn't "two whoops and a holler" away, you "turned your toes to the daisies."

Cowboys loved to exaggerate. A fellow, for example, was not merely tall; he was "so tall he couldn't tell when his feet were cold." If a cowboy wanted you to explain something simply, he would ask you to "chew it finer, please." He had no use for fancy words or the show-offs who spouted them. Fancy words, he would say, "showed up as big as a skinned hoss,"[2] while their user "got calluses from pattin' his own back." But an ignorant person "couldn't drive nails into a snowbank" or "teach a settin' hen to cluck." A delicate person was "so weak he couldn't lick his upper lip."

All this was mild, compared to the cowboy's use of profanity. He boasted of his ability to "cuss a blue streak," without repeating himself or pausing for breath. Swearing, some said, is healthy; it "takes the strain off the liver." His songs were filled with profanity, later omitted by editors of music books so as not to offend the public.

But a cowboy never swore in front of respectable ladies. Women were highly prized in cattle country, because there were so few of them. The cowboy was nearly always a bachelor; he married only when he began ranching for himself or quit the cattle business. If troubled by "Cupid's cramp"—the urge to marry—he might court one of the local girls or seek a mail-order bride. Eastern companies published magazines with pictures and information about women willing to marry and move to the frontier. These were known as "heart-and-hand women," after *The Heart and Hand*, the most popular magazine of its kind.

A good woman, although not always a beauty, was a treasure. She bore children, kept house, and learned to live outdoors. That meant learning to ride horses; riding meant being able to visit neighbors or accompany her husband on trips. "It is not uncommon," wrote a Texas woman, "for ladies to mount their mustangs and hunt with their husbands, and with them to camp out for days. . . . All visiting is done on horseback, and they will go fifty miles to a ball with their silk dresses, made perhaps in Philadelphia or New Orleans, in their saddle-bags."[3] A cow-

A romantic portrait of a real lady

boy who mistreated or insulted such women was in deep trouble. No one in the outfit would speak to him or help him in time of need. And if someone put a bullet into him, well, that was just fine too. The "varmint" had it coming.

Cowboy justice was swift, sure—and permanent. The frontier was so vast that in some places fewer than a hundred whites lived in an area of a thousand square miles. It often took years for the legal system to catch up with the settlers. Until then, there were no written laws, police, courts, judges, or jails. Each man had to protect himself by his own courage and skill with the gun. The six-shooter, therefore, was more than a weapon; it was an instrument of justice. Samuel Colt, its inventor, was hailed as "one of the fathers of American democracy." His gun was known as the "equalizer." "God made some men big and some men small, but Sam Colt made them all equal," was a common saying in the West. Colt pistols had similar mottoes engraved in their barrels. One said: "Fear no man that walks beneath the skies, for I equalize."

The six-shooter was so cheap that practically anyone could afford one. Depending on the model, it cost between twelve and twenty dollars. There were no such things as gun licenses. All men went armed; indeed, boys carried weapons. A boy learned to shoot a gun when he was strong enough to hold it up. The *Southern Intelligencer*, a newspaper printed in Austin, Texas, noted on October 13, 1858: "It is a common thing here to see boys from 10 to 14 years of age carrying about their persons Bowie knives and pistols."[4] John Wesley Hardin, the noted gunman, toted a six-shooter at the age of eight. Ranch women also learned to shoot, since there was no telling when they might have to defend themselves and their children against the Comanche.

The standard six-shooter weighed four pounds and was carried in a holster attached to a belt. A scaled-down version weighed one pound and fit into a trouser pocket; it is said that the hip pocket was invented specifically for that purpose. But whatever the size, a cowboy felt uncomfortable without his trusty "shooting iron." He wore it on the job, in town, and when he went courting; girls expected their beaus to be armed. According to Dr. J. B. Cranfill, a Baptist preacher in Texas, "I would have

Texas gunslinger John Wesley Hardin. Hardin claimed to have killed forty men; most of his victims were unarmed blacks and Mexicans.

The six-shooter carried by John Wesley Hardin when he died

felt much more comfortable going up the street without my trousers than I would have without a gun."[5]

Bullets were valuable in and of themselves. In the Old West, gold and silver coins were far more common than paper money. But since a silver half-dollar was the smallest coin available, it might be necessary to make change to the value of quarters and dimes. Different-size bullets, known as "cowboy change," served this purpose.

Under the cowboy's rules, shooting an unarmed man, or shooting a person in the back, was considered murder and punished accordingly. It was all right, however, to kill in a fair fight or unintentionally during a quarrel. When, for example, a cowboy got drunk or lost his temper, out came his pistol. Bullets flew. Men died. That was too bad, but no one considered it a crime. Yet cowboys were not "shootists," professional gunfighters. Most cowboys were too busy with their own work to practice at becoming quick-draw artists. Basically, the six-shooter was worn not to kill but to protect the wearer's life and property. The vast majority of cowboys never shot anyone.

The cowboy was above all a workman. Although he loved what he did, he did it for pay. The average wage was a dollar a day, about three hundred dollars a year, give or take a few dollars either way. That was good money, compared to others' earnings. Factory workers made about the same, only they lived in cities, where the cost of living was higher, and they had families to support. It was often so difficult to make ends meet that wives and children had to take jobs. Since the cowboy was a bachelor, his money went further. All he had to buy was his own clothing and equipment; food and housing were paid for by his boss, except during winter layoffs. Then he lived off savings and handouts from ranch kitchens. Accepting hospitality from one ranch after another was called "riding the grub line."

Cowboys lived in bunkhouses, log buildings with low ceilings and rough wooden floors. Furnishings were simple: bunks and mattresses filled with straw, a table, some chairs, and a potbellied stove. Apart from these, bunkhouses had none of the comforts of home. They were cold and drafty in winter, and they sweltered in summer. In all seasons they stank of unwashed bodies, dirty clothes, and boots encrusted with cow manure. Brown stains, where someone had missed the spittoon with his chewing tobacco, dotted the floors.

Residents knew bunkhouses by various names: "doghouses," "shacks," "dumps," "dives," and "louse cages." Lice were indeed a plague. They crawled everywhere, into men's bedding, clothes, and hair. Charles Siringo recalled that his bunkmates "made an iron-clad rule that whoever was caught picking gray backs [lice] and throwing them on the floor without first killing them, should pay a fine of ten cents for each and every offense."

In their spare time, cowboys read magazines with articles on fires, earthquakes, and train wrecks. Stories about big-city criminals and western outlaws were always popular in bunkhouses. Where gambling was permitted, men took a chance on almost anything. They played cards, dice, and dominoes. They bet on which of two birds, sitting on a corral fence, would fly first, or who could spit closest to a grasshopper. In louse races, several insects were put on a plate and money bet on which one would crawl off first. Betting on fights between pet tarantulas, hairy spiders the size of your hand, was a pastime on Texas ranches.

Some men had fun with their six-shooters. If, for example, a cowboy used a fancy word, another might shout, "Where'd it go—there it is!" and blaze away at a dark corner where the ornery critter was hiding. Bored cowboys also lay on their backs, popping away at flies on the bunkhouse ceiling. One fellow spent his days off counting and recounting the bullet holes overhead— all 3,620 of them.

During a normal workday, lasting from sunup to sundown, the cowboy rode the range to prevent his boss's livestock from wandering. He doctored sick animals as best he could. Summer was especially hard, since blowflies hatched by the millions in the heat. These insects laid eggs in a scratch or open wound. When the eggs hatched, maggots, or screwworms, bored into the animal, causing dreadful pain and even death. If a cowboy noticed swelling, he opened the area with his knife, scooped out the screwworms, and daubed on a mixture of carbolic acid and axle grease. Horses, on the other hand, had to be kept away from locoweed. Eating this plant made them *loco*, Spanish for "crazy." Once a horse tasted locoweed, it became addicted, just

A cowboy sits in front of the bunkhouse during his time off.

like a person under the influence of drugs. To satisfy its craving, it ate more and more, until it died in agony.

The cowboy himself was hardly a picture of health. Cuts, bruises, sprains, and broken bones were all part of a day's work. There was no escaping them, and everyone had his share, along with the scars they left behind. But since doctors were few and far away, people relied upon home remedies. A sprained ankle, for instance, was wrapped in paper and soaked in vinegar. A treatment for diphtheria was for "the sick person to urinate in a cup of green carrots and hang the cup on the chimney for eight days." To cure acne, you must "wash your face in a baby diaper wet with urine but not feces."[6]

Cuts were treated in various ways. One method was to fill it "with spit or manure," another to "let a dog lick it clean."[7] Chewing tobacco, however, was the preferred treatment. To disinfect a cut on himself or a comrade, the cowboy pulled it wide open, spit tobacco juice into it, and squeezed it until the blood and juice ran out the sides. A bandage was then torn from the patient's shirt, since first-aid kits were unknown on the open range. Crude as they seem, these remedies were common at the time. Soldiers in the U.S. Army used them until they could receive proper medical attention.

Accidental deaths were nearly as common as wounds. There was no telling when someone would be gored or trampled by cattle. If a cowboy fell from his horse and his foot caught in the stirrup, he would be dragged on the ground as the animal galloped across the plains. Western newspapers often carried notices like the following:

A herder . . . named Albert Jones, a few nights ago, became sleepy and tied himself on his horse with his lariat. He was found dead, after having been dragged and jumped over the prairie for a long distance.

W. J. Davis . . . died . . . from the effects of injuries received by being thrown from a pitching horse. Davis was thrown into a bunch of horses and trampled under their feet. He was 45 miles from where he could receive medical attention and was hauled that distance by wagon.

[A] herder was knocked down by a wild steer and his face disfigured for life. His nose was torn completely from his face. That he was not killed was owing to the fact that the long horns, wide apart, touched the ground on either side of the poor fellow's head as he lay prostrate.[8]

The cowboy protected himself as best he could. He watched his animals and studied their ways, always looking for danger signs. He learned to fight thirst by sucking a bullet, make a hearty soup by boiling prairie dogs, and find water by watching swallows: They fly toward water in the morning and away from it in the evening. Every item of his clothing had a definite purpose. It was so practical that, save for minor details, it has not changed in over a century.

The cowboy's hat, modeled upon the Mexican sombrero, gave protection in all weather. When it rained, its wide brim kept his head and shoulders dry; when the sun blazed, it shaded his face. In winter, its high crown insulated the top of his head. The hat was also useful in fanning a camp fire, carrying water, and distracting a charging bull when thrown in its face. A cowboy seldom removed his hat. He wore it indoors, even kept it on when he went to bed. When he did take it off, his forehead was pure white, compared to his suntanned face. The difference in color was so noticeable that, in Indian sign language, the sign for a white man was to pass fingers across the forehead. The "J. B."—for J. B. Stetson—was the best hat you could buy. It cost ten dollars and was guaranteed for a lifetime.

Sears Roebuck sold Stetson hats and complete cowboy outfits.

Around his neck the cowboy wore a bandanna. No mere ornament, this square of red cloth was the unofficial flag of the range country. It had more uses than almost anything else the cowboy owned. As a first-aid device, it made a fine tourniquet, bandage, and sling. In cold weather, it served as earmuffs. In hot weather, it kept the sun from the back of his neck; placed wet under the hat, it cooled his head. In a windstorm, worn as a mask, it kept dust out of nose and mouth. By placing it on the ground and laying his ear on it, the cowboy could hear distant sounds. From this custom we get the saying "Keep your ear to the ground," meaning be alert. In a pinch, the bandanna became a rope to tie an outlaw's hands—or to hang him.

The cowboy seldom wore a coat, because it restricted his freedom of movement. His shirt was made of gray cotton or flannel and had no collar. A vest was worn over it but never buttoned, since that was supposed to cause colds. His favorite pants were Levi's, manufactured by Levi Strauss of San Francisco. Made of heavyweight blue denim with copper rivets to reinforce the pockets, Levi's were both durable and comfortable. Levi's were men's clothes; no self-respecting women wore pants, let alone tight pants. Women wore dresses, even when riding astride, or "clothespin" style. Eastern women, who prided themselves on being more "ladylike," rode sidesaddle, an uncomfortable position in which they sat with both legs on the same side of the horse.

Cowboys seldom wore belts or suspenders, which chafed their skin. They expected pants to stay up by themselves and bought them to fit tight around the waist. Long johns, complete with a "trapdoor" in the rear, were worn under their pants most of the year. Chaps were worn over them when riding in thick underbrush. The whole costume, from coat to chaps, cost less than fifteen dollars.

The cowboy was in his element on horseback. He believed that man and horse were made for each other and that riding was as natural as breathing. "A man on foot is no man at all," westerners said. That was no boast but the plain truth. A man unhorsed on the plains had little chance of surviving. Distances were so great that he might die of thirst or hunger before reaching a settlement. He might be killed by wild animals or captured by Comanche, a fate worse than death. And without a horse he could not earn a living. There was no way to herd longhorns without a horse; indeed, they were so used to seeing mounted men that they charged anyone who appeared on foot.

Horse thieves were the lowest creatures on God's green earth. "It is conceded that the man who steals a horse in Texas forfeits his life to the owner," a newspaper reported in 1878. "It is a game of life and death. Men will pursue horse thieves for five hundred miles, go to any length, spend any amount of money to capture them, and fight them to the death when overtaken. That they will be totally exterminated admits of no doubt."[9]

A captured horse thief was doomed. Either he was shot on

White angora wool chaps

sight or became the guest of honor at a "necktie party"; that is, hung from the nearest tree or telegraph pole. Some, however, were denied even the dignity of a hanging. At least one fellow was dragged to death and his battered body left as a warning to his friends. Another was shown "mercy." Caught in the act, he was given the choice of hanging or having his leg muscles cut. He chose the latter, becoming a cripple for the rest of his life.

In the movies, cowboy stars have their "wonder" horses— big, graceful creatures fast as the wind. Everyone knows their names: Roy Rogers's Trigger, Gene Autry's Champion, Hopalong Cassidy's Topper, the Lone Ranger's Silver. Working cowboys seldom owned a horse; and if they did, it was a small animal worth about twenty dollars. Ranchers often refused to hire men with their own mounts, believing that they would not ride them hard enough to do an honest day's work. Horses were assigned by the ranch foreman and remained the ranch's property. But one horse per man was hardly enough. Since a horse tired after a few hours' work, a cowboy had a string of six to eight mounts. And these were tools, not pets. After seven years of hard riding, the average mount was fit only for the glue factory. During emergencies, horses might be ridden to death.

A workhorse was generally a mustang captured about age four. It was still a wild animal, a bronco with a mind of its own. In order to be useful, it had to be broken. The word meant just that: breaking its will so that it would obey its rider's every command. This was not work for ordinary cowboys, but for specialists who risked their lives each time they got into the saddle.

Horse breakers, or broncobusters, went from ranch to ranch looking for work. Breaking was no joyride, but a brutal struggle. It began when cowboys roped a horse, tied it to a post, blindfolded it, and strapped a saddle to its back. When the broncobuster mounted, they removed the blindfold and undid the rope. Let a veteran cowboy describe what happened next:

> It's all bosh, this talk of cowboys learning to enjoy . . . riding bucking horses. Riding a bucking horse is like having boils— you never get thoroughly used to it. When you hear a fellow say he would like to ride a bucking horse he is either a liar or a greenhorn. . . . I have seen but one man that had grit enough to

Workhorses were tools, not pets—and belonged to the ranch, not to the cowboy.

69

sit a real bucking horse until it had bucked all it wanted to, and he was bleeding at the nose, mouth, and ears when they took him off the horse at the end of a half-hour's struggle. As a general thing a cowboy will pull a horse's head up, wind the reins around the saddle horn, take a firm grip on the saddle with his hands, and then rowel the bucker until the animal becomes convinced that it is better to behave than to buck.[10]

Bronco busting in a print by western artist Frederic Remington. Getting a horse used to a saddle and rider was not work for the ordinary cowboy, but for an expert who was paid extra for this dangerous job.

The Cowboy by Frederic S. Remington
(Amon Carter Museum, Fort Worth, Texas)

Breaking Camp by Charles M. Russell
(Amon Carter Museum, Fort Worth, Texas)

Silver-mounted spurs
*(Buffalo Bill Historical Center,
Cody, Wyoming)*

Falling did not faze an expert rider. "Biting the dust" without breaking his neck was one of the first things a broncobuster learned. He knew how to go limp, hit the ground rolling, and escape the deadly hooves. Yet even the best rider occasionally took a "fartknocker," or hard fall. For each horse broken, the broncobuster received five dollars and the right to give it a name. A horse's name told something of its appearance or personality. If it seemed clumsy, the rider might call it Puddin' Foot. Other names included: Red Hell, Hammer Head, Rattler, Dumbbell, Lightning, Big Enough, Popcorn, Cannonball, Monkey Face, Few Brains, Rat Hash, Texas Terror, Colorado Cloudburst, Dakota Demon, Montana Man-Killer. All of these were stallions. No cowboy or vaquero would ride a she-horse, since that was beneath his dignity.

Proper gear was a must on the plains. A good pair of boots cost twenty dollars and was worth every penny. Boots were for riding, not walking. Their thin soles allowed a rider to feel for the stirrups. Rounded toes permitted him to get his feet into and out of them quickly. Two-inch heels kept his feet from slipping forward through the stirrups. A spur, or "gut hook," was attached to each heel. Plain iron spurs cost five dollars a pair. Silver spurs, engraved with elaborate designs, cost ten times as much. If you owned expensive spurs, you were said to be "well-heeled." A humorist once defined a cowboy as "a man attached to a gigantic pair of spurs."

Last, but not least, came the saddle. This was the cowboy's pride and joy, his most valuable possession in all the world. Since he spent more time sitting than standing, it had to be both sturdy and comfortable. He might skimp on other things, but, if wise, he paid top dollar for a saddle. The best could cost one hundred dollars, five times as much as his horse. It was so important that the saying "He's sold his saddle" took on special meaning in cow country. Anyone who did this was so broke that he had to leave the cattle business. It might also mean that he had lost the respect of his comrades or, indeed, lost his mind.

The busiest time for the cowboy lasted from early spring to midfall. Since cattle grazed on the open range, those belonging

Spurs and saddle as advertised in Sears Roebuck

A cowboy has caught a maverick, an un-branded animal, and tied its legs before branding it and releasing it among his own herd.

to different owners always got mixed together during the winter. Sorting them out was the aim of the roundup, when ranchers joined to gather each other's stock at a central point. During the spring roundup, the more important one, cattle that had drifted away were returned to their owners, calves were branded, and herds were driven to the Kansas cow towns. The fall roundup was to brand calves born in the summer and return any strays that had been missed earlier.

Roundups were complicated operations that required careful planning. As many as twenty ranches might be involved at once, covering an area of five thousand square miles; a Texas roundup of 1885, the largest in western history, covered ten thousand square miles. Each ranch, depending upon its size, sent a work crew to a central roundup camp. Two or three hundred cowboys normally took part, plus two to three thousand horses. Everyone was under the command of a roundup captain appointed by the ranch owners. An experienced cowman whom everyone respected, he was one of the busiest men on the range. "He's a feller that never seems to need sleep," a cowboy moaned, "and it makes 'im mad to see somebody else that does."[11] The captain's word was law, and disobeying his orders meant being barred from the roundup. That was serious, for no one could gather his stock without the help of his neighbors.

Roundups combined work and play. While the captain and owners made final plans, cowboys met old friends, made new ones, and had a good time. There were card games, roping contests, wrestling matches, and practical jokes galore. A fellow would tie a sleeping friend's spurs to a log, then wake him by banging on a frying pan. Another joke was to put smelly Limburger cheese on a sleeping man's mustache. At night, after supper, cowboys sang and listened to stories. As the camp fire burned, sending sparks toward the stars above, someone with the gift of gab stepped into the circle of light and began to speak. He told of his own adventures, or about heroes, real and imaginary. It made no difference if everyone knew the story; what counted was the way it was told. A real storyteller could hold his listeners' attention for hours.

Everyone knew about Pecos Bill, the cowboy superman. By all accounts, when Bill was a baby he fell out of his folks' wagon just after crossing the Pecos River in Texas. Since there were seventeen children in the family, his parents didn't miss him for a month. Though they gave him up for dead, he was rescued by coyotes and raised with their pups. Bill learned everything from Ma and Pa Coyote. When he left them, he was the smartest, strongest, roughest, toughest, fightingest fellow in the West. He invented the lariat, using it to catch soaring eagles, and dug the Rio Grande with a stick. Bill's horse was so ornery that only he could control it, hence its name, Widow Maker. One day Bill's girlfriend, the gorgeous Sluefoot Sue, decided to ride it. Widow Maker threw her so high she had to duck as she zoomed past the moon. Unfortunately, she was wearing a dress with a steel-spring bustle. Each time Sue hit the ground, she bounced back into space. *Boing! Boing! Boing!* She bounced for three days and three nights, until Bill, always a gentleman, shot her to keep her from starving. Bill lived to a ripe age, then he met a tenderfoot from the East. The fellow asked such silly questions that Bill lay down and laughed himself to death.

The roundup began at daybreak. After breakfast, cowboys saddled their mounts and received final instructions. Each had several horses, all specialists at a given task. Roundup horses were swift, sturdy animals, ideal for chasing cattle. Where others hesitated, they plunged into thick brush to drive cattle into the open. Cutting horses separated—cut out—individual cattle from the herd. A good cutting horse knew as much about cattle as its rider. Able to take sharp turns and stop on a dime, it seemed to know what a cow would do before it knew itself. Night horses were used to guard cattle at night; because of their keen eyesight, they could usually avoid prairie-dog holes. A man's most valuable mount was his night horse, and he never used it for any other purpose.

Roundup. A cowboy, lasso ready, moves into the herd to cut out a calf for branding.

The cowboys rode several miles in each direction, forming a circle with their camp at the center. Reaching their assigned positions, they fanned out and began to close in. Slowly the circle tightened, forcing the cattle toward the camp. Already wisps of smoke rose from distant fires, where branding irons glowed cherry red. A longhorn had little hope of escaping, for if it avoided one rider, it came into line with another. Finally, one large herd was formed near the camp.

Now work began in earnest. While the roundup crew held the herd in check, others mounted their cutting horses. Moving swiftly, they separated the cattle according to brand, until several smaller herds, each guarded by its owner's cowboys, were formed. Since calves always follow their mothers, they automatically became a part of each owner's herd. A cowboy had only to ride into the herd and cut out a calf with his lariat. *Baw-w-w-w-w-w*, it bawled, as he dragged it toward a fire.

A four-man team sprang into action. Two cowboys called flankers threw the calf to the ground and held it while a third, the brander, pressed his iron firmly into its left side. Meantime, as an added identification, a fourth man, the cutter, earmarked it by slicing a chunk of flesh out of its ear. To avoid confusion, each rancher had his animals' ears cut in a certain shape. They might be cut off squarely at the top, notched on either side, or

Roundup time. Within minutes, this young male will be castrated, branded, and earmarked for identification.

Rocking chair

Lazy S

Barbecue

John Chisum's Long Rail

Halff's Quién Sabe
(Don't know)

Terrapin

"jinglebobbed"; that is, cut partially down the middle, causing the lower halves to flop around. Brands are difficult to see when cattle are crowded together in herds, but both ears are always pointed forward. This allows a rider, as he moves through a herd, to find his animals easily. Finally, nearly all bull calves were castrated to help them gain weight and make them easier to handle. A castrated bull is called a steer and cannot mate with a female. Only a few choice bulls were kept intact for breeding purposes.

Branding was the main form of identification. Since there were so many ranches, it required imagination to invent an original brand. Various designs were used, such as the anvil , stirrup ♉, rocking chair ♫, scissors ✂, hat ⌂, and bow and arrow ♉. Letters, singly or in combination, were also favored. Let's use the name *Marrin* as an example. If several ranchers' names began with the letter *M*, it could take various forms to avoid mix-ups. That letter with a line on top became the bar M M̄ ; or on each side, the bar M bar-M-; given "wings" atop each arm, it was the flying M M ; with "legs," the walking M M ; with curves at "arms and legs," the running M M; with a "rocker" beneath, the rocking M M ; inside a square, the box M M ; and "too tired to stand by itself," the lazy M Σ. Some ranchers had a sense of humor. Texan T. J. Walker branded his cattle with FOOL, indicating "a man's a fool to raise cattle." Another adopted the 2 ♋ P brand. Translation: "too lazy to pee."

No matter what the brand, putting it on hurt. As soon as the iron met flesh, the calf bellowed. Cowboys understood its pain; many carried scars where an iron had slipped and touched them for an instant. The scars were not pretty, and there was nothing romantic about getting them. "I told one fellow," cowboy D. J. O'Malley recalled, "if he would sit with his bare skin on a red hot stove for a minute he could form a pretty good idea as to how a calf felt when a hot iron was putting a brand into his side."[12]

The work continued without letup. Each team worked under the midday sun, the smell of sweat, blood, and burned hair hovering in the air. On average, three hundred calves could be branded, earmarked, and castrated in a day. When one part of the range was cleared, the roundup camp was moved, and the process repeated as often as necessary. In the end, only the "dogies" remained; a dogie was an orphan, or "a calf who had lost his mamma." These were distributed among the ranchers in proportion to the size of their herds. When all cattle were accounted for, cowboys drove them back to their home ranches.

Most were then turned loose to roam freely for another year. A certain number were selected for the Long Drive to Kansas. Even today, people who may know little else about the Old West have heard of the Long Drive. To see how it worked, we must invite ourselves on a "typical" journey up the Chisholm or Western Trail about the year 1875. Although our drive never took place exactly as described, it has elements in common with all of them.

Ranchers did not necessarily make the trip in person; it took three months to go from San Antonio to Abilene or Dodge City, and they had responsibilities at home. It was easier to turn stock over to a drover, someone who arranged cattle drives for a living. The drover operated in either of two ways. He might buy cattle from several ranches on his own, or agree to take a herd to market, sell it, and share the profits with its owner.

Once the drover had a herd, he assembled a trail-driving outfit. A trail boss was hired at $125 per month, a princely sum in those days. An expert cowman, the boss was responsible for

A trail boss relaxes for a moment. He was the most important member of the cattle-driving outfit—and the highest paid. He planned each day's drive and saw that everything moved smoothly.

➤➤➤   77

the herd's safe delivery. He selected each day's route, scouted the trail, located water, and chose the campsite. During the day, he rode ahead of the herd, communicating with his men from a distance. He would ride to a hilltop, if one was nearby, and signal his orders. Signals were made by waving his hat or arms. Certain signals, borrowed from the sign language of the Plains Indians, were later adopted for use by the deaf.

The trail boss helped the drover select a work crew. As a rule, one cowboy was needed for each 250 to 300 head of cattle. Since herds averaged between 2,000 and 3,000 animals, the outfit had eight to twelve cowboys. Experience showed that larger herds were more difficult to manage. The largest herd on record, 15,000 animals, left Texas in 1869 and had more problems than normal. Films that depict tens of thousands of cattle trampling across the plains are pure fiction.

Next to the trail boss, the cook was an outfit's highest paid member. Known as the Old Lady, he was often an older cowboy who had given up the horse for the chuck wagon. This vehicle was invented by Charles "Chuck" Goodnight, owner of the first ranch in the Texas Panhandle. In 1866 Goodnight converted a surplus army wagon into a rolling storehouse and kitchen. It

The chuck wagon was the domain of the cook. Not only did "Cookie" see that the cowboys were fed, he made all important decisions in the absence of the trail boss.

carried everything the outfit needed; it had to, for once across the Red River, there were no stores for hundreds of miles. Cowboys' bedrolls and extra clothing rode in the wagon body, along with boxes of bacon, jugs of vinegar, and canned goods. Spare harness, horseshoeing equipment, and a toolbox were kept in separate compartments. A barrel with a two-day supply of water was attached to the outside. In the rear was the chuck box, a cupboard with drawers for flour, sugar, plates, and bottles of "medicinal" whiskey.

Nobody kept longer hours than the Old Lady. First to rise, at 3:00 A.M., he was the last to bed, sometimes turning in after midnight. Not only did he prepare meals, he was a jack-of-all-trades. He doctored wounds, pulled teeth, sewed buttons, cut hair, and gave advice. If the boss was away and a decision had to be made, he made it. But it was his food that could make or break a trail drive. Good "grub" kept cowboys happy and keen; poor food made them grumpy and lax. That gave the cook tremendous power, and men were always careful to stay on his friendly side. Those who did not were doomed to short rations at mealtime.

The last member of the outfit was the wrangler. Like so many western terms, it comes from the Spanish; a *caballerango* is "one who cares for horses." The wrangler looked after the herd of workhorses, which might number as many as 150 animals. And, of course, that herd also had a special name. It was the remuda, from *remonta*, Spanish for "remount."

The wrangler knew every horse by name and could tell at a glance if any were missing. If so, he had to find them, even in the middle of the night with wolves on the prowl. A wrangler

The wrangler at work with the remuda

was usually a teenager learning to be a cowboy, and he received half the regular wage. Yet he was every inch a horseman. When eighteen-year-old Jess Langdon was asked about his riding skills, he snapped: "I can ride anything that's got hair on it!" Jess later joined the U.S. Cavalry.

Trail bosses tried to start early in the spring, since the first herds to leave had the best grass to eat. At the beginning, the bosses set a pace of twenty-five miles a day for three or four days. This was to move the cattle away from familiar country as quickly as possible; cows get homesick and will turn back if given half a chance. Once clear of the home range, the pace slowed to ten miles a day. Speed was never the object of a cattle drive. "When cattle run," says a Texas proverb, "they run off tallow." And tallow is money, because they are sold by weight. The aim, then, was to go along at a leisurely pace, allowing the cattle to get plenty of food and rest. If all went well, they weighed more at the end of the drive than at the beginning. Only the men exerted themselves.

Each day's drive followed a set routine. Shortly before daybreak, the Old Lady woke the outfit. If he was considerate, he did so gently. "Arise and shine and give God the glory!" he'd call, or recite a cheerful poem:

Bacon in the pan,
Coffee in the pot!
Get up an' get it—
Get it while it's hot!

But if he was a grouch, he'd yell, "Damn your souls, get up!" and threaten to throw the food away.

As each man came to the chuck wagon, he took a tin cup, tin plate, knife, and fork, and received the traditional trail breakfast: bacon, beans, biscuits, and coffee. Cowboys were the world's star coffee drinkers. There was always a steaming pot of it at the camp fire. No milk or sugar for them! That was sissy stuff. They demanded their coffee full strength; that is, "hot as hell, black as sin, and strong as death." The best was called "six-shooter coffee," because it was "thick enough to float a pistol." Weak coffee was "belly-wash," unfit for human consumption.

Breakfast over, the drive got under way. A herd did not move as a solid mass, but as an elongated wedge, pointed in front and widening toward the rear. This was because cattle, like people, have their own personalities. The moment they hit the trail, the most aggressive animal took the lead and kept that position throughout the drive. Behind him came the less aggressive, the young, the weak, and the lazy.

The rear of the chuck wagon contained a cabinet for cooking utensils, spices, flour, medicines, and "medicinal" whiskey. The cowboys' sleeping rolls were carried in the body of the chuck wagon.

Morning roundup. Each morning, the wrangler got the remuda ready for the day's work. Even after being broken, the horses might resent going to work. The one shown here certainly did.

Men were positioned at key points in relation to the herd. Out in front rode the cook in his chuck wagon. Off to the side was the wrangler and his remuda. Behind the chuck wagon, a few hundred feet away, came the outfit's two most experienced men. Known as point men, they led the herd, guiding it in the right direction. Swing men rode on either side of the wedge, spaced at intervals to prevent animals from dawdling or breaking away. Drag men brought up the rear, nursing along the stragglers. This was the least desirable position, since it meant riding in dust clouds for hours at a time. Drag men put their bandannas over their faces, but these were of little help. They "ate dust," feeling it crunch between their teeth. They coughed and wheezed; some had their eyesight ruined by the constant irritation. No wonder cowboys said the drag was the best place to learn cuss words.

After they had gone about five miles, it was noon, time for lunch. While the herd rested, the men ate in shifts. Lunch was potluck, anything the cook had available—and coffee. An hour later the drive continued until five o'clock, or until it reached the bedding ground. Selected by the trail boss, this had plenty of water and grass. While the cook prepared supper, guards allowed the herd to graze until nightfall.

Meanwhile, the cowboys had supper. This was their main meal, and the cook went all out. Beef was the preferred dish, and any stray cow that had joined the herd, or any one lame from the drag, was fair game. But if these were unavailable, they had to settle for bacon; healthy cattle were too valuable to eat on the trail.

The Old Lady cut thick steaks, dipped them in flour, and fried them in tallow. The rest of the animal was used in son-of-a-gun stew, the cowboy's favorite dish. "You throw ever'thing into the pot," a cook explained, giving his recipe, "but the hair, horns, and holler." Tongue, liver, heart, kidneys, brains, and other organs were cut up and mixed together. The mixture was seasoned with salt, pepper, Louisiana hot sauce, and marrow gut, the half-digested contents of the tube connecting the cow's four stomachs. Everything was then cooked for three hours and more spices added. Dessert might be canned tomatoes or pies made with dried prunes, raisins, or apples.

After supper, those not on guard duty gathered at the camp fire. They spoke softly, or perhaps someone played his harmonica; few cowboys owned guitars, and those who did left them behind, since there was no spare room in the chuck wagon. But it had been a long day, and tomorrow would be no different.

Eating dust. Following the rear of the herd was dry, dirty work for the cowboy.

➤➤➤ **83**

Cowboys bedding down for the night. Trail herding was not glamorous, as may be seen from the men's clothing.

Men's eyelids drooped, and they began to nod off. One by one, they went to the chuck wagon for their bedrolls. These were simply a rubberized ground cloth and one or two woolen blankets. Removing their hats and boots, they slid under their blankets, their saddles serving as pillows. Anyone without a bedroll was said to have a Tucson bed; that is, he lay on his back and covered it with his belly.

Few cowboys had a full night's sleep on the Long Drive. Since there were no tents, they lay exposed to the elements. If the temperature fell, they shivered. If it rained, they got soaked. Crawling things worried even the bravest men. A cowboy poet explained:

How happy I am when I crawl into bed,
And a rattlesnake rattles his tail at my head,
And the gay little centipede, void of all fear
Crawls over my pillow and into my ear.

Centipedes, or "hundred-leggers," were inquisitive critters, and they stung. A rattlesnake might slither under a man's blanket and snuggle up to him for warmth. More than one fellow was bitten when he woke up and startled the reptile. The only thing to do then was to cut into the wound with a knife and suck out the poison. Cowboys believed that circling a bedroll with a lariat kept rattlesnakes away. Perhaps. Perhaps not.

Many dangers had to be faced before a herd reached its destination. Indians were the least of them. The Chisholm Trail lay east of Comanche country, and they seldom gave trouble. Nor did the tribes of the Indian Territory: Cherokee, Choctaw, Creek, Chickasaw, Seminole. These tribes, known as the Five Civilized Nations, had been forced off their lands in the Southeast and settled in the Indian Territory before the Civil War. Peaceful farmers, they asked ten cents for each animal that crossed their reservations. Some cattlemen refused to pay, and six-guns barked. But that did not happen often; for here, at least, the U.S. Cavalry protected Indian rights.

The worst dangers were natural, not man-made. Depending upon where a drive began, it might have to cross several wide rivers. On the Chisholm Trail, for instance, there were the Colorado, Brazos, and Red rivers in Texas; the Canadian and Cimarron in Indian Territory; and the Arkansas in Kansas. Calm during most of the year, they became raging torrents when the snows melted in the Rockies. Worse, they might overflow their banks, forming pools of quicksand. Any cow or man trapped in quicksand was a goner.

Longhorns were fussy about crossing rivers. They refused to

An easy river crossing. The water is low and the current slow moving, making it easy to drive the herd across safely. Getting cattle across a river required enormous skill and luck. The animals might easily panic and go into a "mill," causing many to drown.

enter the water with the sun in their eyes, or if they could not see the far shore. But once in, they were powerful swimmers. Except for their heads and horns, they seemed to vanish. The scene reminded one cowboy of "a thousand rocking chairs floating on the water."

Nevertheless, disaster lurked nearby. A wave, a whirlpool, or floating brushwood might panic the leaders. They would turn around and head back, becoming mixed up with those swimming behind. The herd would begin to mill, this is, move in an ever-tightening circle as more animals pressed in from the sides. The mill grew tighter, tighter, pushing under those in the center.

Cowboys had to work fast to break up a mill. They would ride into the tangle, striking the animals to get them back on course. One brave fellow would leap onto the back of a cow, then move from cow to cow until he'd reached the center, where he turned the leaders in the right direction.

Delay meant a disaster involving hundreds of animals. In 1879 a herd of 3,014 steers panicked while crossing the Platte River in Nebraska; 800 were lost before the mill could be broken. Men might be lost as well, gored or thrown from their mounts in midstream. The lucky ones managed to grab a horse's tail and be pulled to safety. If not, they drowned; strange as it may seem, many cowboys never learned to swim. Every riverbank held the graves of drowned cowboys.

The Night Herder by Frederic S. Remington
(Buffalo Bill Historical Center, Cody, Wyoming)

Cowboy hat, circa 1900
*(Buffalo Bill Historical Center,
Cody, Wyoming)*

The Lee of the Grub Wagon by N. C. Wyeth
(Buffalo Bill Historical Center, Cody, Wyoming)

A Bronc to Breakfast by Charles M. Russell

Bronco Buster by Charles M. Russell
(Buffalo Bill Historical Center, Cody, Wyoming)

Weather presented different problems. During dry spells, entire herds went blind from lack of water. Prairie fires swept the plains, moving so rapidly as to overtake men on galloping horses. A man caught in a prairie fire was known as a "fried gent." Hailstorms, on the other hand, dropped chunks of ice the size of chicken eggs. There was no place to hide out there, under the big sky. Birds and jackrabbits were pelted to death. All a man could do was dismount and cover his head with his saddle.

Nothing compared to a stampede for sheer terror. Longhorns were restless by nature. During drives, a few always turned out to be troublemakers. These spooked easily and tried to run, taking others along with them. The troublemakers received special treatment. Charles Siringo says that his outfit tied their hind legs or even sewed up their eyelids, to keep them in line. It took two weeks for the thread to rot, allowing the eyes to open. By that time, the cow was "broke in." If not, it wound up as son-of-a-gun stew.

Cowboys were especially watchful at night, when stampedes were most likely to occur. To keep awake, night guards took a "rouser"—rubbed chewing tobacco juice inside their eyelids. To calm the herd, they sang. Cattle enjoyed singing, chiefly slow, sad ballads. Not that they understood the words; rather, the sound itself had a soothing effect. Singing was so important that some trail bosses refused to hire anyone who couldn't carry

Cowboys always dreaded stampedes. Anything might spook a herd, from a prairie dog to the rumble of distant thunder. To halt a stampede, cowboys had to head off the herd leaders and start them moving in a circle.

a tune. Among the favorites were "Green Grow the Lilacs"; "When You and I Were Young, Maggie"; "Darling, We Are Growing Old"; "The Dying Cowboy"; and "Bury Me Not on the Lone Prairie." Both cowboys and cows liked the song "Jesse James," about the "lad that killed many a man," and of his killer, "that dirty little coward," who "ate of Jesse's bread and slept in Jesse's bed," then "laid poor Jesse in his grave."

Nevertheless, cattle were light sleepers. Anything might rouse them with a start: the scent of a skunk, a coyote's howl, the rattle of a cook's skillet, a cowboy striking a match to light a cigarette. Cattle even saw ghosts and had bad dreams, cowboys believed.

Lightning usually triggered a stampede. The Great Plains, being flat and open, were extremely dangerous during electrical storms. Long before the storm arrived, the sky blackened and the air became still. As it approached, the wind picked up and thunder echoed in the distance. Lightning came in every shape and form. Sheet lightning, forked lightning, and chain lightning turned night into day. Cowboys, fearing that metal would attract the deadly bolts, threw away spurs, knives, and six-shooters. Swearing stopped, since that might provoke God's anger. Everyone, said John Connor, a nineteen-year-old wrangler, was scared. "The horses bunched together around me, stuck their heads between their knees and moaned and groaned till I decided the end of time had come. So I got down off my horse and lay flat on the ground and tried to die, but could not."[13] Others died easily, killed in a flash of blue light and a puff of smoke. Lightning was one of the most common causes of death of the Long Drive.

A stampede was a nightmare come true. Instantly, as if someone had flipped a magical switch, the herd sprang to its feet and started running. The pounding of thousands of hooves woke the soundest sleeper. "Everyone up!" the trail boss shouted. Leaping from their bedrolls, his men mounted their night horses and took off after the herd.

Halting a stampede took skill, courage, and luck. Except when lightning flashed, the night was so dark that men couldn't see their hands in front of their faces. Prairie-dog holes were everywhere, waiting to snag a horse's foot. A false step would send horse and rider head over heels.

Gradually, men drew alongside the herd leaders. The intense

body heat of the herd could blister men's faces. Yelling and firing their pistols close to the leaders' ears, they tried to make them change direction. Yet this could not be done at once, for three thousand cattle build up momentum as they run. Bringing them to a sudden halt, even had it been possible, would cause a pile-up in which hundreds would be crushed or suffocated. The object was to turn them into a circle, forming a mill. Then, as the mill grew, the stampede would slow down until it stopped entirely.

Even so, a stampede was never without cost. At the very least, animals lost weight, up to fifty pounds in a four-mile dash. At most, lives were lost. The worst stampede occurred in 1876, when a herd plunged into a gully near the Brazos River, killing 2,700 steers within minutes.

Men also died. Teddy Blue tells what happened to one of his friends. They found him at daybreak, beside his dead horse. "The horse's ribs were scraped bare of hide, and all the rest of horse and man was mashed into the ground as flat as a pancake. The only thing you could recognize was the handle of his six-shooter. We tried to think the lightning hit him, and that was what we wrote his folks down in Henrietta, Texas. But we really couldn't believe it ourselves. . . . I'm afraid his horse stepped into one of them [prairie-dog] holes, and they both went down before the stampede. We got a shovel—I remember it had a broken handle—and we buried him nearby. . . . But the awful part of it was that we had milled them cattle over him all night, not knowing he was there. . . . And after that, orders were given to sing when you were running with a stampede, so the others would know where you were."

The drive continued northward, ever northward. Its novelty had long since worn off. It was no longer an adventure. The same faces, the same grub, the same dangers made every day the same as every other. Bored and tired, men fell silent. Even old-timers felt the strain. Tempers grew short, and the boss had to order all six-guns stowed in the chuck wagon.

Then, when least expected, the mood changed. A stagecoach appeared on the horizon. Or the wind brought the hoot of a train whistle. "Hey, Pete, hear that?" a point man asked his partner. Pete smiled. Others had heard it too. Everyone was smiling. The end of the trail was in sight. Soon they would be paid off and go to town.

CHAPTER FOUR

Going to Town

"You strap on your chaps, your spurs, and your gun—
You're goin' to town to have a little fun."

—*Cowboy song*

MAIN STREET, A KANSAS COW TOWN IN THE EARLY 1870S A
bright autumn day with a gentle breeze blowing across the
plains.

It is high noon, but the street is deserted, save for two men
coming toward each other from either end of town. They walk
slowly, deliberately, spurs jingling on their heels. As they pass
each building, eyes follow them from behind curtains. Mothers
push inquisitive youngsters under heavy pieces of furniture.
Merchants tremble behind shop counters and barrels. Gamblers
watch intently from the saloons that line both sides of the street,
taking bets on the outcome. This is the showdown, and only
one of the rivals will live to see another sunset.

Each has an equalizer in a holster at his side. There is no
doubt as to who is who. Our hero wears a white hat, symbol of
purity and devotion. He is the town marshal. His opponent
wears a black hat, symbol of the evil rotting his soul. He is a
desperado with "credits," notches cut into the handle of his
weapon.

Two shootists fight it out in this illustration by Remington.

Closer they come, closer, each watching for the other to make the first move. Black Hat scowls defiantly, as if looks could kill. White Hat is not disturbed a bit. His expression, steady as the man himself, never changes. His step never falters. He is determined that justice shall be done today.

Suddenly Black Hat reaches for his gun. He *is* fast, but not fast enough. Like greased lightning, White Hat draws and fires once. That is all it takes—one shot. Black Hat clutches his chest and goes down, dead before he hits the ground. Justice has prevailed.

This is a familiar scene, the climax of innumerable western films. Though shoot-outs are dramatic, and everyone loves a hero, movies seldom (if ever) give an accurate picture of the Old West. To learn why, we must see what the Kansas cow towns were actually like, and what cowboys did when they visited them.

Abilene or Dodge City seemed like a bustling metropolis to the cowboy, even though during their heyday, each had fewer than twelve hundred permanent residents. When the trail herds arrived, though, the population instantly doubled and tripled. Thousands of cowboys camped around the town, eager for an opportunity to cut loose.

A view of Front Street in Dodge City during the 1880s. This was the town's main street, where cowboys came to drink, gamble, and meet the "soiled doves" in the dance halls. Note the sign prohibiting the carrying of guns. Thanks to its efficient police department, Dodge City was not nearly as dangerous as it was portrayed in Hollywood movies.

Cow towns were similar in appearance. Shops lined the main street, their prices specially raised for their visitors' benefit. Each building was one story high but had a false front to give the appearance of height. Streets were unpaved, forcing merchants to build sidewalks outside their shops. These were eight feet wide and made of rough wooden planks. In the rainy season, the street became a quagmire. In the dry season, it was a dust bowl. A gust of wind, a galloping horse, a moving freight wagon, or cattle bound for loading pens raised clouds of dust. Streets lay ankle-deep in cow and horse manure, a menace to women with long, ground-sweeping dresses. Manure was bad enough when it baked in the sun, and its odor got into everything. But when it dried, it turned to a fine powder that blew into people's faces, houses, and food. Our cities today, jammed as they are with automobiles, smell sweet by comparison.

Towns had no water supply other than nearby rivers and hand-dug wells. River water was not necessarily pure; besides being muddy, it might also carry wastes from cows grazing upstream. You could dip a glass into a river and watch manure particles dart every which way until they settled to the bottom. People disposed of garbage wherever they pleased, and instead of indoor plumbing, there were backyard outhouses. These were frigid in winter, but even worse in summer, when flies swarmed and the odor became unbearable.

If your home caught fire, your neighbors came running with buckets since there was no fire department, fire engines, or fire pumps. Barrels of water were placed at intervals along the sidewalks in case of fire.

When a herd arrived in town, it was sold and the cowboys were paid off. Each cowboy then had about a hundred dollars, in cash, and he knew what he wanted. It wasn't whiskey or a good time—at least not right away. He wanted to be clean. After three months on the trail, he looked like a beggar and smelled like a horse.

The cowboy's first stop was the haberdasher's for a new set of clothes. But it made no sense to put clean clothes on a dirty body. So, with the parcel tucked under his arm, he went to the nearest barbershop for a haircut and, luxury of all luxuries, a bath. Barbershops had bathtubs, and for twenty-five cents he could soak in hot water as long as he wished. Clean again, he

Painting the Town Red, by Frederic Remington. At the end of a long drive, cowboys enjoyed a few days in town, buying new clothes, taking a bath, gambling, and carousing with the dance hall girls.

might join his pals at the town photographer's for a group picture. Hundreds of these pictures survive, valuable sources of information about cowboy life.

After having worked so hard, most cowboys felt entitled to a little fun. Their idea of fun, however, was not reading poetry. Cowboys wanted action; they called it "going on a tear" and "smoking up the town." That meant, for some, giving the rebel yell while galloping their horses on the sidewalks, shooting into the air, and putting holes into water barrels. It meant watching the tenderfeet dance; that is, making townsmen hop around by shooting bullets near their toes.

Frightening as this may seem, there seems to be no instance of a "dancer" being hurt, let alone killed. Nor did all cowboys act up. Joseph McCoy tells us in his book *Historic Sketches of the Cattle Trade of the West and Southwest* that plenty of them stayed out of trouble, saved their money, and later went into business on their own. Some were religious men and made a beeline for church their first Sunday in town.

This Remington drawing shows a tenderfoot "dancing."

Nevertheless, townspeople were not amused by the cowboys' antics. Guns were fearful things to them, and those who used them seemed like wild men. Besides, the Civil War was still a vivid memory. Cowboys, we recall, were mainly Southerners, while Kansans were Yankees; "Damnyankees" and "Bluebellies," cowboys called them. During the war, Quantrill's Raiders, a band of rebel guerrillas, had burned the town of Lawrence, Kansas, slaughtering 150 men, women, and children. Among the raiders were the James boys, Frank and Jesse, and Cole and Jim Younger, soon to follow the outlaw trail.

Once again, Kansas was being invaded by rebels—and by Texans at that. General Philip Sheridan expressed their mood in a wisecrack: "If I owned hell and Texas, I'd live in hell and rent out Texas." A Texan replied, "Bravo for Sheridan. Damn a man who won't stand up for his own country."[1] But Sheridan had made his point: Texans were not popular in Kansas.

That left townspeople with a dilemma. They disliked cowboys, but they also needed them. Cowboys had money and spent it freely. As a result, the town allowed cowboys to have fun, charged them for the privilege, and tried to keep them under control. It is this combination of resentment and greed, fear and contempt, that shaped the history of the Kansas cow towns.

Every town had its cowboy section, usually near the railroad tracks. Respectable folks lived on one side of the tracks—"the right side." On "the wrong side" were the saloons, gambling dens, dance halls, and shabby hotels. Saloons were always profitable; towns had twice as many of them as any other business. Dodge City had nineteen saloons and twelve hundred residents; that is, one saloon for every sixty-three people. Owners gave their places colorful names like the Alamo, Lone Star, Last Chance, Bull's Head, Do Drop In, Applejack, Pearl, and Lady Gay. Dodge City's Long Branch saloon later became famous in the television series "Gunsmoke." The only similarity between TV's Long Branch and the real thing was the name; otherwise, the TV version was a complete fraud.

Rough places that catered to rough men, saloons were anything but glamorous. A bar, thirty to forty feet long, occupied a whole side of the building. On the wall behind it was a large mirror and rows of bottles. The other walls had life-size paintings

of women in scanty costumes and "daring" poses. Kerosene lamps hung from the ceiling, over gambling tables covered in green cloth. Sawdust was strewn on the floor, to soak up any chewing-tobacco juice that missed the spittoons. The place reeked of tobacco juice, spit, smoke, liquor, horse liniment, and sweat. Men's talking and laughter mingled with the clinking of glasses and music from brass bands and pianos that played round the clock.

Saloons served hard liquor. Before the railroad, barrels of raw alcohol came by wagon. The saloonkeeper diluted it with water, colored with coffee, and flavored with black pepper; to

After being paid off, cowboys gather in a saloon to drink whiskey and beer.

give added "bite," he might toss in a dead rat or snake. It was called "rotgut," from its ability to eat away one's stomach. Rotgut was so strong, cowboys said, that it could "draw a blood blister on a rawhide boot." Other names for liquor were "bug juice," "coffin varnish," and "tanglefoot."

Once the railroad tracks reached town, wines and liquors could be brought from the East. So could beer, which cowboys preferred ice-cold. To satisfy them, saloonkeepers built storage sheds insulated with bales of straw. During the winter, they cut blocks of ice from frozen rivers and piled these in the sheds, which cooled the beer far into the summer. When the ice finally melted, more was brought by train from the mountains of Colorado.

Drunken cowboys were a common sight in town. Alone or in groups, they roamed the streets after dark, firing their six-shooters and yelling at the tops of their voices. They might even ride their horses into a saloon and up to the bar to demand more whiskey. At daybreak, they returned to camp with aching heads and sour tastes in their mouths.

Gambling went hand in hand with drinking. Saloons either hired professional gamblers to play for the house or invited them to play on their own in return for a share of their winnings. Thousands of dollars crossed the gaming tables each night during the cattle season. The most popular games were keno, similar to bingo; chuck-a-luck, played with dice; faro, whose object was to guess the next card to be drawn from a pack; and various other card games.

Poker was the cowboy's all-time favorite. He could spend an entire day at the poker table without getting bored. His love for the game has enriched the American language in ways we seldom recognize. Expressions like "bluffer," "I call your bluff," "cash in," "lay your cards on the table," "showdown," "turn it down," "passing the buck," "ace in the hole," "rotten deal," and "square deal" were originally cowboy poker terms.[2] Yet few cowboys could say that poker ever enriched them. To be sure, many sold their saddles during all-night poker games.

Cheating began where skill and luck ended. A dishonest gambler knew how to mark a deck or pull a card out of his

Thousands of dollars crossed the tables each night in towns such as Abilene and Dodge City.

sleeve. If a cowboy objected, there was a good chance of his leaving the table feetfirst. Not only did gamblers play cards, many had reputations as gunmen. They usually packed a Derringer pistol, also called a pocket cannon. This tiny terror was five inches long and fired only two shots. Derringer users seldom drew on anyone—they simply shot through the pocket.

Gamblers realized that, good as they were, there was always someone just a little bit better. This lesson, however, might have to be learned the hard way. One day a fellow arrived in Dodge City dressed as a minister. The "Reverend" saw no problem with gambling, since God always looked after His own. And he surely was one of God's own. Whenever he gambled, he began with a prayer for divine favor. He won game after game, until an ace fell from his sleeve. But not to worry; he could explain everything. He had not put the card there, said he, without blinking an eye. The good Lord put it there to enable him to punish sinners. He left town in a hurry, vanishing without a trace.

Another time, a youngster in torn work clothes wanted to try his luck at poker. He knew nothing about the game, he claimed, but had a little money to wager. The gamblers smiled broadly and invited him to sit down, son. The youngster fumbled with the cards, asked how to shuffle and deal—but took every pot. Beginner's luck? Certainly not. The humorist Mark Twain was right: "You can't tell how far a frog can jump just by looking at him."[3] Only later, after the youngster left town, did they learn that he was a professional who specialized in tricking other gamblers.

Dance halls relieved the cowboy of his remaining money. Every town had its dance hall; Dodge City had two, one reserved for whites, the other open to whites and blacks alike. But whatever their color, cowboys took dancing seriously. Joseph McCoy saw them in top form:

> Few more wild, reckless scenes . . . can be seen on the civilized earth than a dance-house in full blast in one of the many frontier towns. To say they dance wildly . . . is putting it mild. The cowboy enters the dance with a peculiar zest, not stopping to [remove] his sombrero, spurs, or pistols, but just as he dismounts from his cow-pony so he goes into the dance. A more odd, not to say comical, sight is not often seen than a dancing cowboy; with the front of his sombrero lifted at an angle of fully forty-five degrees; his huge spurs jingling at every step or motion; his revolvers flapping up and down like a retreating sheep's tail; his eyes lit up with excitement and liquor, he plunges in and "hoes it down" at a terrible rate, in the most approved yet awkward country style; often swinging his "partner" clear off the floor for an entire circle, then "balance all" with an occasional demoniacal yell. After dancing furiously, the entire "set" is called to "waltz to the bar," where the boy is required to treat his partner, and, of course, himself also, which he does not hesitate to do time and again. . . .[4]

"DANCE-HOUSE."

Their dancing partners were not local women. Drifters, they came for the cattle season, returning to New Orleans or Chicago when the cowboys left. They went by nicknames like Lil Slasher, Wicked Alice, Fatty McDuff, Peg-Leg Annie, Toothless Nell, and Big Nose Kate. Known as "soiled doves" and "calico queens," they were different from the women cowboys respected. Calico queens were hardly "ladylike" and had police records to prove it. They cursed, fought with knives, and kept Derringers in their garters. Instead of regular wages, they received part of the money charged for each dance—seventy-five cents for ten minutes—plus a share of the profits from the bar. For additional fees, they entertained cowboys privately in the tiny bedrooms at the rear of the dance hall.

Abilene was the rowdiest of the cow towns. During its heyday, it attracted all sorts of characters. Gandy dancers, buffalo hunters, and mule skinners drank deeply and fought fiercely in the

At a dance hall in Abilene, Kansas, from a drawing in Joseph G. McCoy's *Historical Sketches of the Cattle Trade*. The sign on the wall advertises "bitters," herbs used in mixed drinks.

➤➤➤ *101*

city of the plains. Then there were the common criminals: murderers, burglars, holdup men, swindlers, rustlers, horse thieves. Many of these were graduates of that great school of killing, the Civil War. War had changed them forever, giving them a twisted view of the world. It taught them that human life was cheap and that violence solved any problem. If they wanted anything, they need only draw a six-gun and take it.

Men such as these mingled with the cowboys in Abilene. Its wildness impressed even John Wesley Hardin. A Texan by birth, he killed more men in gunfights than anyone else in American history; alongside him, Billy the Kid and Jesse James were amateurs. Hardin killed forty men between his fifteenth birthday and his capture ten years later, in 1878; he once shot five armed men in under a minute. "I have seen many fast towns," he recalled, "but Abilene beat them all. The town was filled with sporting men and women, gamblers, cowboys, desperadoes, and the like. It was well supplied with barrooms, hotels . . . and gambling houses; and everything was open."[5]

That is an understatement. For a time, Abilene had no law at all. When the cattle drives began, it was still a frontier settlement, not an organized town with a government. Legally, it was not entitled to public services or even to a police force. People, in order to protect themselves, formed "vigilance committees." Vigilantes were like volunteer fire departments. They were ordinary citizens who tended to business as usual, but they sprang into action at the first sign of trouble.

Vigilantes found one fellow with a murdered man's belongings. They hanged him at a mill outside Abilene. They must have been very quiet, since Mrs. Florence Bingham, who lived nearby, only learned of it at breakfast the next morning. "[The] school children came running past our house, all excited," she recalled years later. "They were going to see the man who was still hanging at the mill. They seemed to think it quite a lark and swung him back and forth by his toes. I could have seen him from my front gate, but I certainly did not want to."[6]

Vigilante "justice" solved nothing. By taking matters into their own hands, vigilantes became judge, jury, and executioner rolled into one. They acted so fast that there was no time to gather all the evidence or pause for reflection. A posse might

Old Ramon by Frederic S. Remington
(The Metropolitan Museum of Art, Thomas J. Watson Library, Rogers Fund, 1901)

Evening at the Round-Up Camp, Montana by Laton Alton Huffman
(The Metropolitan Museum of Art)

be excused for hanging a murderer, but there was no guarantee that this would always be the case. Sooner or later, an innocent person would be killed by mistake. Only a government could bring law and order.

In September 1869 Abilene's leading citizens, including Joseph McCoy, formally created a town to be governed by an elected council. The council promptly made it a crime to carry guns inside the town limits. Additional laws were passed to license saloons, gambling houses, and dance halls. A courthouse and jail were built. Tom Sheran, a grocer, was appointed town marshal to enforce the laws.

Judging from the movies, marshals fought single-handedly against the forces of evil. Not so. Towns never depended upon one lawman. The marshal was "captain of police," head of a five-man team. (A sheriff was the peace officer in a county, which included several towns.) Serving under him was a deputy marshal and three policemen. In addition to law enforcement, the marshal saw that the streets were kept in repair, inspected chimneys for fire hazards, and supervised garbage removal. In one town, he was expected "to arrest swine found at large." The marshal also kept order in court, arresting "any person caught throwing turnips, cigar stumps, beets, or old quids of tobacco" at the judge and jury.[7]

Marshal Sheran had his hands full from the outset. There was no problem in collecting license fees; saloon owners paid these gladly. Cowboys, however, resented the gun law and told him so to his face. Signs prohibiting guns were shot to pieces. The jail was torn down. When it was rebuilt, cowboys tore it down again, freeing its only inmate, a trail cook arrested for drunkenness. For good measure, they emptied their six-shooters into the mayor's office as they rode back to camp. That was the last straw. The marshal, fearing for his life, handed in his badge and returned to his grocery store.

Who would be the next marshal? It was not just a matter of finding the right man for the job, but also the right *kind* of man. There were those who wanted a "shootist," a professional gunfighter. Shootists were a breed apart. A common criminal, or a cowboy, might be an excellent shot, but he was helpless against a shootist. Not only did the professional shoot straight, he was

Marshal Tom "Bear River" Smith brought law and order to Abilene, not with a gun, but with his fists.

a master of the quick draw. It was plain suicide for an ordinary person to challenge a shootist.

Shootists, however, were not the most reliable people. Most had little regard for human life and might break the law whenever it suited their purposes. At least two became marshals to conceal their criminal activities; another was killed while holding up a stagecoach. Even if honest, a shootist could bring more trouble than he prevented. The presence of a gunfighter attracted glory hunters. Killing a marshal, even by shooting him in the back, made them "big men" in the frontier underworld. But if the marshal killed them, their friends might come seeking revenge. Either way, there was bloodshed.

In June 1870 Abilene hired Tom "Bear River" Smith as marshal at a salary of $150 a month. The son of Irish immigrants, Smith had been a policeman in the Bowery, New York City's toughest neighborhood. After the Civil War, he went west to make a career as a peace officer. He earned his nickname while breaking up a riot in Bear River, Wyoming. A solid, muscular man with blue-gray eyes and a soft voice, he didn't smoke, drink, gamble, or use foul language. Though he carried two six-shooters, he wore them under his coat, out of sight. Bear River Tom did not trust guns, nor did he need them—not when he had two hard fists.

Smith's first act was to post signs in the saloons and gambling houses: ALL FIREARMS ARE EXPECTED TO BE DEPOSITED WITH THE PROPRIETOR. Then he mounted his horse, Silverheels, and set out to enforce the law.

The marshal's first run-in was with a cowboy called Big Hank. A big bully with a big mouth, Big Hank was not about to part with his shooting iron. When Smith asked him to turn it in, he became nasty. "Are you the man who thinks he's going to run this town?" Hank snarled. Meantime, a crowd had formed, expecting to see the marshal back down or be shot down.

"I've been hired as marshal," said Smith firmly. "I'm going to keep order and enforce the law."

"What are you goin' to do about the gun ordinance?" Big Hank asked.

"I'm going to see that it is obeyed—and I'll trouble you to hand me your pistol now."[8]

No way! Instead of handing it over, Big Hank let loose a flood of curse words. He never finished his sentence. Instantly, Smith's right fist shot forward, catching him squarely on the jaw. Down he went. The marshal grabbed Hank's gun, hauled him to his feet, and ordered him out of town. Big Hank meekly obeyed, never again to set foot in Abilene. He had been totally humiliated.

Smith's tactic had taken everyone by surprise. A feature of any cowboy movie is the grand fistfight, accompanied by flying chairs, crashing mirrors, and bodies sprawled on the barroom floor. "We don't know no more about fistfightin' than a hog knows about a sidesaddle," said a cowboy as Big Hank stumbled out of town.[9] He was right. Fistfighting was something strange and awful to cowboys. As southerners, they had never learned to use their fists. Boxing was considered ungentlemanly in the South. Gentlemen settled their disputes with pistols or daggers. Being punched in the face, knocked into the dirt, and disarmed was the worst indignity a cowboy could suffer. Smith had used a "secret weapon" cowboys did not understand. And that in turn added to his reputation as a lawman.

By sundown, news of Big Hank's disgrace was the talk of every saloon and cow camp. In one camp a cowboy, Wyoming Frank, vowed to make the marshal beg for his life on hands and knees.

Next morning, Wyoming Frank rode into Abilene with two six-shooters at his sides. Dismounting, he stood in the street outside the Lone Star Saloon, waiting for the marshal to appear. Smith was still at breakfast, but Wyoming Frank boasted that he had scared him out of town.

Just then, Bear River Tom came walking down the middle of the street. The cowboy cursed him at once, spat on the ground, and dared him to go for his guns. Instead, Smith asked for his weapons, while looking him straight in the eye. That gaze seemed to bore through the bully, and he began to back away. But with each step backward, the marshal came closer, closing the distance between them. This was not merely a test of wills, but a precaution on Smith's part; for the closer he came, the less room his opponent had for drawing a gun.

Wyoming Frank retreated backward, through the doors of the

Lone Star, and up to the bar. Unable to retreat any farther, he made his move. But he was no gunfighter. Smith let him have a "one-two"—a punch in the stomach to double him up, then one to the chin to straighten him out as he fell. "I give you five minutes to get out of town," said Smith, taking away his guns. "And don't you ever again let me set eyes on you." Like Big Hank, Wyoming Frank left without a murmur.[10]

Everyone was astonished. Once again, Bear River Tom had enforced the law without firing a shot. The owner of the Lone Star stepped from behind the bar and handed over his pistol. "That was the nerviest act I ever saw," he said. "You did your duty, and the coward got what he deserved. Here's my gun. I reckon I'll not need it as long as you're marshal of this town." With that, his customers turned in their six-shooters as well. Smith told them to check them with the bartender until they were ready to leave town. Abilene had met its master at last.[11]

Bear River Tom became a figure larger than life. Respect for those dreadful fists became respect for the man behind them and the law he represented. Now and then a cowboy arrived without knowing that things had changed. Smith straightened him out fast enough. The worst was over, and no one died of gunshot wounds during his time in Abilene. But in November, after five months of service, Smith was killed while arresting a farmer for murder over a land boundary. The farmer lived in a shack outside of town. As the lawman entered the shack, the farmer's friend hit him from behind with an ax, chopping off his head. He had just turned thirty.

Abilene mourned its hero. The whole town turned out for the funeral and collected money for a monument to his memory. It read:

> THOMAS J. SMITH
> MARSHAL OF ABILENE, 1870
> DIED A MARTYR TO DUTY NOV. 2, 1870
> A FEARLESS HERO OF FRONTIER DAYS
> WHO IN COWBOY CHAOS
> ESTABLISHED THE SUPREMACY OF LAW

Truer words were never carved into stone.

After Smith's murder, citizens worried that Abilene might not find a suitable replacement. But in the spring of 1871, as the herds came up the Chisholm Trail once again, a man known as Wild Bill applied for the job. Six feet two inches tall, weighing 165 pounds, he had a shaggy mustache and brown hair that reached down to his shoulders. He stood erect, constantly moving his head from side to side, his blue eyes studying everyone and everything. His hands were delicate, almost feminine, with long, tapering fingers. Every so often he patted the two pistols tucked into a red sash around his waist.

James Butler Hickok—to give his true name—was born in Illinois in 1837. A restless youngster, at eighteen he went to Kansas, where he supported himself by farm work, gambling, and driving a stagecoach. While working on a government wagon train, he ran some thugs out of a small town. He had done the citizens a favor, and they were grateful. "Good for you, Wild Bill!" a woman shouted, blowing him kisses. We do not know why she used that name, but he liked it. From then on he was Wild Bill Hickok.

When the Civil War began, Wild Bill joined the Union army as a scout. After the war, he hunted army deserters for the reward and became marshal of Hays City, Kansas. He was not popular in Hays City and, after a quarrel with off-duty soldiers, left town in a hurry. When asked why, he said, modestly: "I couldn't fight the whole Seventh Cavalry." A few days later, on April 15, 1871, he became marshal of Abilene. His salary was $150 a month, plus a share of the fines collected from those he arrested and fifty cents for every unlicensed dog he shot. Rabies was a problem, and dogs without collars were shot as a safety measure.

Wild Bill Hickok was a second-rate man and a first-rate gunfighter. When not gambling, he courted the calico queens; he lived with one woman after another, leaving them when he became bored. He distrusted everyone. Fearful of being ambushed from a doorway or alley, he seldom used Abilene's sidewalks; instead, he walked in the middle of the street, his hands on his guns. Indoors, he sat with his back to the wall, never to a door or window. He was especially cautious at bedtime. Before turning in, he spread crumpled newspapers on the

James Butler Hickok, otherwise known as Wild Bill, was dismissed as marshal of Abilene after killing two men, one his own deputy.

floor to wake himself if anyone entered the room. He took a six-shooter to bed and, as an added precaution, kept a sawed-off shotgun on his night table. During the night, he awoke several times to check the security arrangements. If things did not feel quite right, he sat till dawn in a chair, the shotgun on his lap, staring into the darkness.

If Hickok was fearful, he had only himself to blame. Killing, he told a newspaper reporter, did not bother him. It was effortless, just something he did when necessary. "As ter killing men, I never thought much about it," he said. "The most of the men I have killed it was one or t'other of us, and at such times you don't stop much to think. And what's the use after it's all over?"[12] Wild Bill boasted of having killed at least a hundred men. That was a tall story; the exact number is uncertain, but it could not have exceeded a dozen. Nonetheless, hundreds would have gladly shot him in revenge or to make their reputations.

Wild Bill may have been the best marksman in the West. Those who saw him in action said he always hit the target dead center, or close to it. He could clip the brim of a hat as it spun in the air or keep a tin can dancing along the ground. He could toss a silver dollar and blow it apart in midair. Once he hung a piece of paper on a fence post; it had a dot in the center, which he hit twice, and put four other holes within an inch of it. Like most shootists, he did not use both guns at once. It is virtually impossible to fire both guns accurately; the second gun was kept in reserve, in case the first ran out of ammunition or misfired. Nor did he cut a notch into the handles of his guns for each of his victims.

Hickok never fought a face-to-face, Hollywood-style duel. A duel is a contest in which opponents are closely matched. Gunfighters did not fight duels with equals, much less give them an even chance. Fighting an equal was risky and best avoided. John Wesley Hardin, for example, visited Abilene while Hickok was marshal. Hickok had Texas warrants for his arrest but ignored them. Hardin, who despised Yankee lawmen, would not challenge the marshal. In effect, they had an unspoken agreement to ignore each other for their own good. So long as Hardin stayed out of trouble, Hickok would not go after him. So long as

Hickok let him alone, Hardin kept out of trouble.[13] Hickok even looked the other way when the Texan wore his weapons in town.

Wild Bill, like all gunfighters, believed in survival at *any* cost. Where their own lives were concerned, there were no rules, no codes of honor, no ideas of fair play. A gunfighter drew fast, shot first, and aimed to kill. If you wanted to live, you had to get the other fellow before he drew, not overtake him after he made his move. Weapons experts today have proven that the man who begins the draw is sure of winning by approximately half a second. The point, then, was not to outdraw an opponent fairly, but to take him by surprise and make the first shot count.

A shootist did not automatically aim for the head or heart. True, a bullet in either spot was fatal, but because these were higher up on the body, they were harder to hit at the moment a gun cleared its holster. It was best to aim low. As Hickok told a friend: "Charlie, I hope you never have to shoot any man, but if you do shoot him, [shoot him] in the guts near the navel; you may not make a fatal shot, but he will get a shot that will paralyze his brain and arm so much that the fight is all over."[14] Sometimes, when a man went down in this way, the winner ran over to finish him with a bullet in the head. Shootists, after all, were killers, not sportsmen.

Hickok's police methods differed from those of Tom Smith. Whereas Smith had patrolled the streets regularly, Hickok stayed in the Alamo saloon, playing poker. Wild Bill seldom went anywhere except to eat at a nearby restaurant, visit a lover, or turn in for the night. His deputies did the legwork, sending for him if they needed help. But this did not happen often. His reputation inspired fear, and troublemakers "walked wide"— kept out of his way.

Two men were killed during Wild Bill's time in Abilene, and he shot them both. A dance hall girl named Jesse Hazel had become his lover. Jesse, however, proved to be fickle. After several weeks, she took up with Phil Coe, a Texas gambler. Hickok was not a good loser. When he saw them together, he knocked Jesse down and kicked her in the face. He and Coe would have gone at each other then and there, had bystanders not interfered. Coe later threatened to kill the marshal. Hickok, for his part, vowed to take care of the Texan first.

Matters came to a head in October 1871. The cattle season had ended, and Coe was preparing to return to Texas with some friends; Jesse had already gone ahead. Before leaving Abilene, Coe and his friends decided to have one last fling. They went from saloon to saloon, getting happier, and drunker, by the minute.

Wild Bill was at his usual place in the Alamo when a shot rang out in the street. Leaping to his feet, he ran to see what had happened. He found twenty Texans and Coe, a smoking revolver in his hand.

"Who fired that shot?" asked the marshal, as if he didn't know.

"I did!" said Coe, explaining that he had fired at a stray dog.[15]

It is unclear what happened next. Some witnesses said Coe then raised the gun and fired at Hickok; others said that he did nothing of the sort. In any case, Hickok put a bullet into Coe's stomach, wounding him fatally. But just as Coe went down, Hickok heard a man running behind him in the shadows. Without hesitating, he whirled around and fired, killing the newcomer instantly. Only then did he discover that it was Mike Williams, one of his deputies. Williams had heard the ruckus and come to help.

Abilene's citizens now saw Wild Bill in a different light. In their eyes he was no longer a hero, but a villain. Because of his jealousy and hot temper, two men had died needlessly. Once and for all, the town council vowed to get rid of rowdies, whether they wore badges or not. On December 12, it dismissed Hickok, after eight months on the job, "for the reason that the city is no longer in need of his services." But that was just the beginning. Two months later, Kansas extended the quarantine, closing Abilene to the cattle trade. A new marshal was hired at a salary of fifty dollars a month. There was no need to pay more; for with the cowboys gone, those who preyed on them had no reason to return. Abilene became just another quiet farming community.

After Abilene, Wild Bill served another brief term as marshal of Hays City. He then toured the country as an actor in a theatrical troupe run by his friend Buffalo Bill Cody. Tiring of that, too, he headed for Cheyenne, Wyoming, where he married a widow some years older than himself. But married life did not suit him, either. After a few months, he went on a gambling spree in Deadwood, South Dakota, site of a recent gold strike. August 2, 1876, found him playing poker in the Number Ten Saloon. On that day he broke a key rule: He sat with his back to the door. It was the last mistake he ever made. A glory hunter named John McCall came from behind and shot him in the head. McCall was hung for murder. Before the execution, however, he told why he had not met the shootist face-to-face: "I didn't want to commit suicide." Hickok lived by the gun and died by the gun. In the end, all his gunfighting skills proved worthless.

A drunken cowboy once boarded a train on the Santa Fe line. When the conductor came for the fare, he held out a handful of coins.

"Where to?" the conductor asked.

"I want to go to hell," the cowboy muttered.

"All right," said the conductor. "Give me a dollar and get off at Dodge."

This story, often repeated, may or may not be true. What matters is that Dodge City, in its early days, seemed like hell on earth.

The town began as a buffalo hunters' camp in 1871. Originally known as Buffalo, the name was changed in honor of nearby Fort Dodge and its commander, Colonel Richard Irving Dodge. It soon attracted the usual riffraff of gamblers, calico queens, outlaws, and gunmen. During its first year, it had fewer than five hundred people, twenty-five of whom died violently. The victims, known locally as "stiffs," were buried on a low hill; and since so many had died "with their boots on," it was called Boot Hill.

Whoever you were, wherever you went, death could strike at any moment in Dodge City. One buffalo hunter, no shrinking violet himself, never forgot his visit to a saloon. As he opened the door, he noticed two men standing side by side at the bar. Just then, one drew a pistol, shoved it into the other's ear, and blew his head off. The sight of his blood excited one of the dance hall girls. She "put the palms of her hands down into the blood that was running on the floor, jumped up and down and hollered, 'Cock-a-doodle-doo!' Then she held her hands up and clapped them in front of her, splattering the blood all over her white dress. . . . I just closed the door and went back to bed."[16]

Peaceable folks did not feel safe even in bed. Mrs. Ellen Biddle and her husband, an army major, had to spend a night in a Dodge City hotel. The manager, a six-foot woman with a bowie knife and six-gun in her belt, showed them to their room. It was located directly over the saloon, and the floor was only one board thick. They had barely closed their eyes when shooting broke out in the saloon. The couple clutched each other in terror, praying that bullets would not come through the floor.

Things began to improve toward the end of 1875. On Christmas Eve, a town council was formed to bring order. As in Abilene, the council banned firearms within the town limits. All visitors were required to check their guns at hotels, stores, saloons, and gambling houses; the owners of these places were forbidden to return weapons to drunken men. In addition, hunting knives, firecrackers, cruelty to animals, and public profanity were strictly forbidden. Off-duty soldiers were not to wear "drinking jewelry," rings made from horseshoe nails with the rough nail heads pointing outward. Those who could not pay their fines went to jail, at first simply a well fifteen feet deep. Unlike Abilene, however, Dodge's peace officers were gunfighters from the outset.

Though still a tough place, Dodge City was pretty civilized when the first herds arrived in 1877. Veteran cowboy Andy Adams warned youngsters to behave themselves—or else.

I've been in Dodge every summer since '77, and I can give you boys some points. Dodge is the one town where the average bad man of the West not only finds his equal, but finds himself badly handicapped. The buffalo hunters and range men have protested against the iron rule of Dodge's peace officers, and nearly every protest has cost human life. Don't ever get the impression that you can ride your horses into a saloon, or shoot out the lights in Dodge; it may go somewhere else, but it won't go there. . . . You can wear your six-shooters into town, but you'd better leave them at the first place you stop. . . . Most cowboys think it's an infringement on their rights to give up shooting in town, and if it

The members of the Dodge City Peace Commission sit for a portrait. *Left to right:* Charles Bassett, W. H. Harris, Wyatt Earp, Luke Short, L. McLean, Bat Masterson, and Neal Brown.

is, it stands, for your six-shooters are no match for Winchesters and buckshot; and Dodge's officers are as game a set a men as ever faced danger.

A list of Dodge City peace officers reads like an all-star lineup of six-gun talent. It included, at one time or another, Charlie Bassett, Mysterious Dave Mather, Bill Tilghman, and Tom Nixon. William Barclay "Bat" Masterson was county sheriff; his brother Ed, a Dodge City policeman. These were no-nonsense fellows, and only fools got in their way. Yet they were not angels. Far from it. Most were professional gamblers as well as lawmen. And one—deputy marshal Wyatt Earp—was no stranger to the frontier underworld.

The "Legend of Wyatt Earp" is exactly that—a legend. Wyatt was born in Illinois in 1848. He drifted into Indian Territory in his early twenties. Arrested as a horse thief, he escaped to Kansas, where he made a living as a buffalo hunter and gambler. He was in Hays City during its wild days, and in Ellsworth at its peak as a cattle town. In 1875 he became a policeman in

Wyatt Earp served for a time as a peace officer in Dodge City. While there, he formed lasting friendships with Doc Holliday and Bat Masterson. All three were gamblers as well as lawmen. After turning in his badge, Wyatt also became a small-time swindler and crook.

Wichita but was fired for stealing the fines he collected from saloons and dance halls. Dodge City, however, hired him to assist marshal Larry Deger. Wyatt served four years, less time away for gambling trips into Texas. After Dodge City, he went to Tombstone, Arizona, to join his brothers, Morgan and Virgil, and his friend Doc Holliday, a dentist turned gambler and gunman. There, on October 26, 1881, they killed three men at the OK Corral. Local people called it murder, because, witnesses said, the victims were shot with their hands up. Wyatt fled, to spend his remaining years as a saloonkeeper, cardsharp, and swindler. He died in Los Angeles in 1929.

William Barclay "Bat" Masterson was a jack-of-all-trades. Beginning his career as a buffalo hunter, army scout, gambler, and lawman, he ended up as a sports editor for a New York newspaper.

Dodge City was the high point of Wyatt's career, and Bat Masterson, who knew him well, praised him as a lawman. Wyatt believed there was safety in numbers, and whenever there was trouble, he took along a couple of officers armed with shotguns. Shotguns fire buckshot, which "leaves a mean and oozy corpse." While they kept the offender covered, he pistol-whipped him; that is, struck him over the head with the barrel of a six-shooter. As the offender lay dazed on the ground, the deputies picked him up, dragged him to jail, and tossed him into a cell. Sometimes, just for the fun of it, they robbed him and beat him up again.

Wyatt was involved in only one Dodge City shooting. On July 26, 1878, a cowboy named George Hoyt fired his gun into a theater. Unfortunately (for Hoyt), Wyatt and another policeman came by at that very moment. As Hoyt galloped out of town, they shot him off his horse. One of the bullets struck him in the leg, and he died a few days later of blood poisoning. Wyatt claimed the kill for himself, but there is no way of knowing who fired the fatal bullet. He was a compulsive liar, forever taking credit for others' deeds or inventing stories about his own heroism, and historians have disproved nearly all of his claims.[17] He was a capable police officer but was certainly no town tamer, let alone master of the fast draw.

Much has been said about violence in the Kansas cow towns. If we are to believe movies and popular fiction, townspeople witnessed a killing each night. But a New Yorker, returning from a western trip in 1884, told a different story. There were, he insisted, "many places in our [eastern] cities where I would feel less safe than I would among the wildest cowboys in the West."[18] That was as true then as it is today.

There were killings, and plenty of them, in the early days of each town. *In the early days.* The worst violence always occurred before regular governments were set up and laws put into effect. Once this happened, things calmed down quickly. Westerners were not lawless by nature.

The five leading cow towns were pretty safe, despite cowboys, gamblers, gandy dancers, buffalo hunters, calico queens, and desperadoes. This is confirmed by reports in local newspapers. Abilene, Dodge City, Caldwell, Wichita, and Ellsworth had a total of forty-five killings in the years 1870 to 1885. Killings averaged one and one-half per each cattle season and never exceeded five in any given year. The largest groups of victims were cowboys, nine killed; gamblers, nine; lawmen, six; and farmers, three. Of the total, sixteen were killed by lawmen. Two lawmen died trying to make arrests; three died accidentally; and one was killed in a private quarrel.[19]

Most towns, whether cattle centers or not, chose local, law-abiding citizens as their peace officers. Even those handy with guns rarely used them, and then not to kill. Wild Bill Hickok was unusually violent, an exception to the rule. Bat Masterson was said to have killed twenty-one men in gunfights. He actually killed one, an army sergeant in a fight over a woman, and that did not happen in Dodge City. Wyatt Earp *may* have mortally wounded one man during his career as a lawman. Mysterious Dave Mather killed one man for sure, but Charlie Bassett and Larry Deger killed none. Western lawmen, therefore, were not nearly as deadly as they have been made out to be. As always, law was enforced not through spectacular shootouts, but by firm and regular police work.

CHAPTER FIVE

Conquering the Great Plains

"I was born upon the prairies, where the wind blew free, and there was nothing to break the light of the sun. I was born where there were no enclosures and where everything drew a free breath. I want to die there, and not within walls. . . . I lived like my fathers before me, and like them, I lived happily."

—*Chief Ten Bears of the Comanche, 1867*

FOR HALF A CENTURY AFTER LEWIS AND CLARK'S EXPEDITION, the Great Plains aroused little interest in the young nation. The plains were too dry for agriculture, people said. They were barren, forever a wasteland at the center of the continent.

These ideas began to change in the years leading up to the Civil War. As the railroads were built westward, Americans realized how wrong they had been about the plains. Settlers in Kansas found no desert, but millions of acres of fertile soil. Cattlemen saw an open range for millions of cattle, a land of opportunity larger than even the Lone Star State. Of course, the plains were already inhabited by buffalo and Indians. But these meant little to the newcomers. Civilization, they believed, demanded that both be swept away and the land turned to "useful" purposes. How this came about is one of the saddest chapters in our history.

The Great Plains were the domain of the buffalo, a strange and marvelous creature. Spanish explorers had described it as *un animal feo y fiero*—"an animal ugly and fierce." "They have very long beards, like goats," a Spaniard wrote,

> and when they are running they throw their heads back with the beard dragging on the ground. . . . The hair is very woolly, like a sheep's, and in front . . . the hair is very long and rough like a lion's. They have a great hump, larger than that of a camel. . . . They rub against the small trees in the ravines to shed their hair . . . as a snake changes its skin. They have a short tail, with a bunch of hair at the end. When they run they carry it erect like a scorpion.[1]

The buffalo was the largest wild animal in North America. A full-grown bull stood six feet six inches at the shoulders, was ten feet from snout to rump, and weighed a ton; adult cows were smaller, weighing in at twelve hundred pounds. No one knows how many buffalo there were before the white man arrived. Scientists believe they numbered sixty million when Lewis and Clark set out on their expedition.

Buffalo grazed in herds so vast that we can scarcely imagine them today. Early travelers saw herds of two million animals *at one time*. Their movements shook the earth, and their bellowing made it difficult to get a night's sleep. As late as 1871, Colonel Richard Irving Dodge found his way blocked by a herd while driving his buggy in southern Kansas. It took five days to pass and was fifty miles deep by ten miles wide. And this herd was nothing special, just one of countless others that roamed the plains.

Plainsmen reported herds temporarily drinking small rivers dry. Trains stalled for as long as nine hours while a herd crossed the tracks; it was useless trying to break through the moving wall of flesh. Trains of the Atchison, Topeka and Santa Fe line were attacked by angry buffalo, even derailed. There were so many buffalo that no one, Indian or white, believed they could ever disappear. No matter how many were killed, newborns would easily make up for the loss.

The buffalo had few natural enemies. A tornado might strike with such force that it lifted bulls into the air, then dropped them to earth, shattering every bone in their bodies. Thousands drowned if the ice broke while they were crossing frozen rivers. Wolves hunted the old and the young, the weak and the crippled. An angry buffalo, however, could destroy a wolf with its horns and hooves. Its most annoying enemy was also the smallest. Spring was shedding time, when the winter coat fell out, leaving the buffalo bald until a new coat grew in. The exposed skin, raw and tender, attracted buffalo gnats, tiny flies whose bites felt like electric needles. Clouds of gnats buzzed around the buffalo, making them miserable. To find relief, they rolled in mudholes. The mud dried, covering each of them with a thick crust, much like a knight's suit of armor.

Indians said that everything they needed, except water to bathe in and wooden tepee poles, came from the buffalo. Its hide was tanned and made into robes, blankets, caps, mittens,

The Great Plains tribes depended upon the buffalo. In this picture, taken in 1870, women are tanning buffalo skins to turn them into leather. Buffalo meat is being jerked—dried—on racks in the background.

moccasins, leggings, shields, saddlebags, drums, and the walls of tepees. Tanning was woman's work, as much a source of pride to her as a man's in his hunting ability and courage in battle. A hide was stretched on the ground and daubed with a mixture of water and buffalo brains to cure it and keep it from drying too fast. This went on for ten days, until the skin was soft and pliable. Properly tanned skins could last for years. The best skins were decorated with colorful designs and handed down from generation to generation.

Buffalo hair was twisted into rope and woven into ornaments. Tails became fly swatters; beards decorated clothing and weapons. Horns made excellent spoons, cups, and storage containers. A backbone with the ribs attached became a sled. Sinew, the fiber that connects muscle to bone, was used for sewing thread and bowstring. Bones were shaped into needles, knife blades, spear points, scrapers, war clubs, and awls to punch holes in leather. Hooves were boiled for their glue, used to fasten arrowheads to their shafts. To make a bow, braves glued two ribs together and wrapped them tightly in sinew. These "composite bows" were springier and more powerful than those made entirely of wood.

Buffalo meat has practically every nutrient needed by humans. The best parts were the tongue, ribs, and hump flesh cooked over camp fires. Blood was lapped up warm from the animal's veins; melted fat was drunk by the pint. The liver and kidneys were eaten raw, even by infants in the cradle. Bones were split open and the marrow scooped out. If water was scarce, you had only to kill a buffalo and plunge a knife into its belly. The green juice that squirted out eased thirst as well as any jug of water.

Buffalo intestines were eaten whole, without chewing. White traders learned to eat intestines, or *boudins*, from the Plains Indians. These were a delicacy, and all wanted their fair share. George Frederick Ruxton, an English traveler, once saw two fur trappers start at either end of a coil of raw intestine. It lay between them on a dirty saddle blanket, like a gray snake. "As yard after yard glided glibly down their throats . . . it became a great point with each of the feasters to hurry his operation, so as to gain a march upon his neighbor and improve the opportunity by swallowing more than his just proportion; each at the same time . . . would suddenly jerk back his head, drawing out at the same moment. . . . several yards of *boudin* from his neighbor's stomach . . . and, snapping up the ravished portions, greedily swallowed them."[2] The contents of the intestines, a mush of partially digested grass, enhanced the flavor.

Indians put aside large quantities of buffalo meat for the winter. Meat was best preserved as pemmican. Long strips were hung on racks to dry in the sun and wind. Women then used stone mallets to pound the strips into tiny flakes, packed them between layers of melted buffalo fat, and stored them in rawhide bags called parfleches. The Comanche flavored their pemmican with dried fruits and berries. Pemmican could keep indefinitely, a tasty, high-energy food in any season. It was especially good when eaten with wild honey.

Even the buffalo's dung was valuable. "Buffalo chips" were flat pieces of manure that littered the plains wherever the herds passed. When it rained, chips stayed dry on the inside, making an all-weather fuel to warm a tepee or cook a meal.

Here, too, whites learned from the red man. Pioneers seldom carried enough wood for their cooking fires; nor did cowboys on their trail drives. But buffalo chips were always plentiful. James Linforth, who crossed Nebraska with a wagon train in 1855, noted: "It is a common joke on the plains that a steak cooked on these chips requires no pepper. Young ladies, who in the commencement of the journey would hardly look at a chip, come into the camp with as many as they can carry. The chips burn fiercely and cook as well as wood."[3]

The main buffalo hunt took place in late summer, when the animals were fattest. Each tribe had special ceremonies to attract a herd. The Blackfeet used songs and dances to bring the buffalo closer. The Crow gave a bowl of food to a buffalo skull and sang, "Hooee! Great bull of the prairie, be thou here with thy cow." The Comanche caught a horned toad and asked it to guide them; they believed it would go toward the nearest herd when released. After a hunt, the buffalo were thanked for their kindness in allowing themselves to be killed by Wakan Taka's children.

The first buffalo hunters, as we have seen, went on foot. Since

A buffalo jump. Before the coming of the horse, Indians killed buffalo by stampeding them over cliffs.

they could not outrun their prey, they had to outsmart it. In Montana, where the Yellowstone River flows between steep cliffs, they hid behind mounds of earth near the edge of a cliff. When a herd approached, they jumped up screaming and waving blankets, stampeding hundreds of animals to their deaths. Over the years, piles of bones accumulated at the base of these cliffs, or "buffalo jumps."

Another method was to approach a grazing herd from downwind, crawling slowly through the grass. Though the buffalo had poor eyesight, it could sniff an enemy a mile away if the wind was right. The slightest hint of man-scent would stampede a herd in the opposite direction. Hunters often draped themselves with buffalo skins, complete with the head and horns, to get close enough to use their bows and arrows. During the winter, if they were lucky, they killed buffalo trapped in snowdrifts.

The horse enabled the red man to hunt at high speed. A hunting party, approaching from downwind, would surround a group of animals. When their leader gave the signal, they whipped their mounts into a gallop. Yelling and shooting arrows, they rode among the buffalo, hoping to kill as many as possible in the shortest time. The buffalo stampeded, trying to break out of the circle of death. Bulls, wild-eyed and snorting with rage, turned on their attackers with their horns.

The horse enabled the Plains Indians to follow the buffalo herds, guaranteeing them a regular food supply. To identify his kill, each hunter marked his arrows with his own special design.

The buffalo didn't have a chance. Hunters were trained from childhood to make every arrow count. They did not aim for the heart; buffalo, like longhorns, could run hundreds of yards with their hearts shot through. Nor could an arrow in the head penetrate the thick bones. But a hit in the lungs brought a quick end.

A dying buffalo was not a pleasant sight. According to Frederick Ruxton, it knew it would die if it lay down. Therefore, it fought desperately to stay on its feet:

> A bull, shot through the heart or lungs, with blood streaming from his mouth, and protruding tongue, his eyes rolling, bloodshot, and glazed with death, braces himself on his legs, swaying from side to side, stamps impatiently at his growing weakness, or lifts his rugged and matted head and helplessly bellows out in conscious impotence. . . . Gouts of purple blood spurt from his mouth and nostrils, and gradually the failing limbs refuse longer to support the ponderous carcass; more heavily rolls the body from side to side until suddenly, for a brief instant, it becomes rigid and still; a convulsive tremor seizes it and, with a low, sobbing gasp, the huge animal falls over on his side . . . [a] mountain of flesh without life or motion.[4]

At first, whites were not very interested in the buffalo. Unlike cowhide, which could be turned into leather, buffalo skins were too soft for most purposes. The only market was in buffalo robes and tongues, but it was small and employed few people. Buffalo robes were used as blankets in buggies and sleds during the winter. Buffalo tongues were served in fancy restaurants.

Even this small market changed the Indian way of life. Indians took their products to trading posts to exchange them for tobacco, beads, mirrors, knives, axes, and cloth. Greedy whites, caring only for money, broke the law and gave them guns and ammunition. It was whiskey, however, that brought the largest profit. Known as "Indian whiskey," it made the cowboy's rotgut seem mild. A typical recipe called for a barrel of water, two gallons of alcohol, strychnine—both a poison and a stimulant—three packages of chewing tobacco, five bars of brown soap, and a half-pound of red pepper. This mixture was boiled to a deep brown color, then strained through cheesecloth.

Hide yard in Dodge City, 1874

Whiskey became the curse of Indian life. Traders deliberately got tribesmen drunk to cheat them out of their goods. Worse, drunken braves went wild, saw dreadful visions, and even murdered their own families. When whiskey appeared in camp, wives took their children and hid on the prairie. The craving for whiskey drove Indians to kill more buffalo than they needed for food. George Catlin once arrived at a trading post at the same time as a Sioux hunting party. The Sioux threw down fourteen hundred buffalo tongues, asking only a few gallons of whiskey in return. They had left the rest of their kill to the coyotes.

The railroads brought death to millions of the shaggy beasts. Gandy dancers built up huge appetites during a day's work. Since buffalo were there for the taking, companies hired professional hunters to supply their needs. Hunters held contests to see who could kill the most within a given time. The champion was William F. Cody, a former army scout. Cody would ride alongside a stampeding herd and fire his Springfield, a lightweight rifle, at close range. He earned the nickname Buffalo Bill by killing four thousand animals within a few months.

Railroads also brought tourists and "sportsmen" to buffalo country. This began soon after Joseph McCoy staged his Wild West show to advertise Abilene as a cattle market. Companies, eager for extra profits, whipped up interest in the buffalo. For ten dollars, they offered the thrill of a lifetime, minus any danger to the thrill seeker. Killing, indeed, was both safe and effortless.

The railroads ran special cut-rate tours for hunters. Here, they enjoy the "sport" of shooting buffalo from a train. The animals were not eaten, but left to rot. In certain places, the plains glittered as the sun reflected off acres and acres of bleached bones.

As trains chugged along slowly, passengers fired repeating rifles from windows. When herds crossed the tracks, bringing them to a halt, people scampered to the car roofs and blazed away until their gun barrels became too hot to hold. Wherever the trains passed, they left vast open-air graveyards in their wake. Both sides of the tracks, for hundreds of miles, were lined with rotting carcasses and skeletons.

This slaughter angered the Indians. The buffalo, they felt, were the Great Spirit's gift to his children. By killing them, the "palefaces" insulted God and threatened their own way of life. If the buffalo disappeared, the red man must also disappear or give up his freedom. He would no longer be himself, but an imitation white man. He would be a farmer, a grubber in the earth, or a beggar living on strangers' charity.

The southern Plains tribes decided to fight while they still had the strength. One by one, they took to the warpath. White hunters were themselves hunted down and killed. Railroad construction crews were attacked so often that rifles had to be kept alongside picks and shovels. Tracks were torn up and telegraph poles cut down. A war party of Southern Cheyenne once derailed a freight train, burned it, and wiped out its crew.

The government heard their message loud and clear. In October 1867, a peace commission arrived at Medicine Lodge Creek in southern Kansas. There it met the chiefs of five leading tribes: Comanche, Southern Cheyenne, Kiowa, Arapahoe, Apache. After long debates, some of them quite bitter, they agreed to a treaty. In return for peace, white hunters were to be barred from the plains south of the Arkansas River. So long as the buffalo roamed, only Indians could hunt in that area. The commissioners spoke for the president, the Great White Father in Washington. Their voice was his voice, their promises his promises. And so it would be till the end of time.

The Treaty of Medicine Lodge proved to be worthless. In 1871, Abilene's last year as a cattle town, whites discovered how to turn buffalo hide into leather for shoes, belts, furniture, and other items. Suddenly hides were selling for $3.50, half of what a cowboy earned in a week. Treaty or no treaty, hunters flocked to Kansas. The buffalo was doomed.

Using Dodge City as a base, hunting teams of from three to twelve men fanned out across the plains. The team boss was the hunter. Slowly he crept behind a rock or clump of grass downwind from a grazing herd. He did not have to get close, thanks to his weapon. The Sharps rifle was a high-powered gun designed for killing buffalo. Although it had to be reloaded after each shot, its killing power was awesome. It could drop an animal at six hundred yards, which made Indians say that it "shoots today and kills tomorrow." A good man with a Sharps was worth his weight in gold. For that reason we still call expert marksmen "sharpshooters."

Sharpshooters turned killing into a science. The idea was to make a "stand"; that is, to keep the buffalo in one place without scaring them away. At first the hunter studied the herd, searching for the leader, normally an old bull. A bullet in the lungs brought him down. Those nearby, attracted by the smell of blood, came over to the body. They milled around, sniffing, staring,

Slaughtered buffalo awaiting
the skinner's knife

bawling. Another bullet, and another buffalo fell, blood pouring from its nostrils. The others gazed in wonder, not knowing what to make of this weird behavior. All they could see was a fallen buffalo and, perhaps, a puff of smoke hanging over a distant clump of grass. If an animal took fright and began to run, it became the next victim. If several ran off at once, the hunter fired quickly, dropping these new leaders in their tracks. The others turned back, only to die in turn. Compared to the hide hunters, Buffalo Bill, the famous hunter and showman, was an amateur. Tom Nixon, the future lawman, killed 120 at one stand in forty minutes; in a one-month period he killed 2,173 buffalo. But the all-time killer was J. Wright Mooar, with 20,500 in less than nine years of hunting.

The skinners began where the sharpshooter left off. Moving quickly, they turned a carcass on its back and drove an iron spike, three feet long, through its head to keep it from rolling over. Using curved, razor-sharp knives, they slit it down the belly and inside each leg. Another cut was made around the neck and the hide loosened from the underlying flesh. One end of a rope was then tied to a corner of the neck skin, the other to a horse. The horse was whipped, and the hide yanked off with a single jerk. The day's haul was taken to camp, pegged to the ground until dry, and sold at Dodge City for shipment to tanneries in the East. On any given day, mounds of hides fifty feet long by six feet high stood beside the tracks. Yet only one hide in three was usable. The rest were either ruined by careless skinners or by insects during drying.

Buffalo hunting was a nasty occupation. Men went months without washing, their clothing stiff with dried blood, their bodies stinking of sweat and filth. Lice, or "graybacks," tortured them day and night. To find temporary relief, they threw their clothes on anthills and let the ants eat the pests. A camp song told of life on the buffalo range:

> Our meat it was buffalo hump and iron wedge bread,
> And all we had to sleep on was a buffalo robe for a bed;
> The fleas and graybacks worked on us, O boys, it was not slow.
> I tell you there's no worse hell on earth than the range of the
> buffalo.

Their earnings, however, made up for their discomfort. Sharpshooters easily earned a hundred dollars a day; skinners, twenty dollars. And, like the cowboys, they went to town for a good time. Dodge City was their favorite spot, and they enjoyed it mightily. They also liked Fort Griffin, Texas, home of Mollie McCabe's Palace of Beautiful Sin, a combination saloon, gambling house, and dance hall. Hunters, their pockets bulging with money, spent everything in a single night of "fun." The money that was the result of such bloodshed in the end served no good purpose.

Within three years the buffalo disappeared from Kansas. Where once they had roamed in their millions, only carcasses and bones littered the ground. Travelers said they could walk a hundred miles in certain areas without stepping off the remains. The smell of death was everywhere, hovering in the air or borne on the winds. By the spring of 1874, the hunters were moving south, into the Texas panhandle. It was a full-scale invasion, and it had not gone unnoticed.

Late in June, the Comanche invited the Kiowa and Southern Cheyenne to a war council on Elk Creek, a branch of the Red River. The council fire blazed, shooting sparks into the night

Opposite: The son of a white captive and a Comanche war chief, Quanah Parker led his people against the buffalo hunters.

sky. Warriors, streaked with paint and wearing feathered bonnets, sat cross-legged, waiting for the speakers to begin.

One by one, chiefs stepped into the circle of light. Stone Calf of the Southern Cheyenne warned that, unless they acted at once, the buffalo would disappear. Kicking Bird of the Kiowa told of the palefaces' broken promises and contempt for Wakan Taka. Little Wolf of the Comanche spoke last. A famous medicine man, he told of a dream-visit to Wakan Taka in the world beyond the clouds. He had given Little Wolf a message for his children. He did not want them to become like the paleface. He wanted them to take to the warpath and kill every white person they could find. If they obeyed, the spirits of the slaughtered buffalo would take new bodies and return to the plains. The tribes, Little Wolf continued, should have no fear, since the Great Spirit had given him the power to turn aside enemy bullets.

At daybreak on Saturday, June 26, 1874, seven hundred braves left camp. The Comanche, the largest group, were led by Quanah Parker. Quanah (Fragrance) was the son of Cynthia Ann Parker, a white girl kidnapped in Texas at the age of nine. Raised as a Comanche, she married a renowned warrior and had three children by him; according to custom, they took their mother's family name. Quanah, their eldest, was born in 1845. Brave and intelligent, he followed in his father's footsteps. Upon turning eighteen, he became war chief of the Quahadi Comanche, the tribe's largest band.

Their destination was Adobe Walls, a hunters' camp in the Texas panhandle just south of Indian Territory. Its main building was a saloon made of adobe bricks, sunbaked clay hard enough to stop any bullet. Nearby was a store and a blacksmith's shop, also of adobe. There were twenty-eight men in the camp, including Bat Masterson, who would later become a lawman.

Next morning, before dawn, a roof beam in the saloon broke with a sharp *snap*, waking everyone at Adobe Walls. With sunrise so near, one of the hunters decided to get an early start. While watering his horses at a nearby stream, he happened to glance toward the horizon. There, in the dim light, he noticed a dark shape moving to the west. It came on steadily, fanning out into a half-circle. As it drew near, he made out a large body

of horsemen. They were painted in gaudy colors and wore feathered bonnets. They carried spears, bows and arrows, and rifles. Many had clumps of hair attached to the bridles of their horses. Scalps.

"Indians!" he shouted, firing his pistol to alert the others. The hunters sprang to their feet and dashed to the saloon, a natural fort.

The *boom* of Sharps rifles mingled with the *crack* of the Indians' lighter weapons. The first casualties were two whites, trapped in a wagon parked next to the saloon. But from then on, the defenders had the upper hand. Sharpshooters all, they fired often and well. Warriors toppled from their horses with gaping holes in their chests. Quanah Parker was everywhere, fighting, shouting encouragement, and helping the wounded. A Comanche, lying near the saloon door, thought he was a goner until Quanah appeared. As bullets kicked up the dust near the injured man's head, he saw the chief ride into the line of fire. Without slowing down, Quanah leaned over, lifted him with one arm, and carried him to safety.

Braves lost faith in the man who had promised them victory. Little Wolf, the medicine man, did not take part in the battle. Completely naked, his body painted yellow, he sat on his horse, praying. That was too much for one warrior. "If the white man's bullets cannot hurt you," he cried, pointing to the saloon, "go down and bring back my son's body." The medicine man refused. His magic, he explained, was gone, and it was the braves' own fault. Moments before the attack, someone had killed a skunk, angering the Great Spirit. It was a lame excuse, and from then on Little Wolf was shunned. Still, nothing could bring back the dead. The raiders left after three days, carrying away fifteen bodies. Twelve others could not be recovered without further loss of life. Before burying them, the whites cut off their heads and stuck them on poles.

Indian anger boiled over after Adobe Walls. In the weeks that followed, war parties ranged across Texas, New Mexico, Colorado, and southern Kansas. No white was safe, least of all a buffalo hunter. Approximately 190 whites died during these attacks.

Last of the Buffalo by Albert Bierstadt
(Buffalo Bill Historical Center, Cody, Wyoming)

Fort Laramie by Alfred Jacob Miller
(Thomas Gilcrease Institute, Tulsa, Oklahoma)

Whites, however, had no intention of giving up. For years they had believed that the red man was a savage who did not deserve this rich land. The Topeka, Kansas, *Weekly Leader* spoke for many when, in 1867, it described Indians as "miserable, dirty, lousy, blanketed, thieving, lying, sneaking, murdering, graceless, faithless, gut-eating skunks as the Lord ever permitted to infect the earth, and whose immediate and final extermination all men . . . should pray for."

Adobe Walls was the last straw. There would be no more peace commissions. From then on, the U.S. Army would deal with the Indians. Its mission was to break the southern Plains tribes, particularly the Comanche, once and for all.

The army was led by ruthless men. William Tecumseh Sherman, its general-in-chief, and Philip Sheridan, his deputy, had made their reputations during the Civil War. Rebels despised

General William Tecumseh Sherman burned the city of Atlanta, Georgia, during the Civil War. After the war, he commanded the army in the West, where he threatened to make war upon the Indians if they did not give up their lands and go to live on reservations.

them, and with good reason. Sherman had destroyed entire cities in his march across Georgia and the Carolinas; Sheridan had burned Virginia's Shenandoah Valley, the "garden" of the Confederacy. Both men believed in total war. Victory, they insisted, meant not only defeating the enemy's forces but making his people suffer so much that they begged their government for peace. "The people," Sheridan explained, "must be left nothing but their eyes to weep with over the war."[5]

The Indians would weep for two reasons. First, the buffalo would be exterminated to cut off their food supply. Second, the army would drive them from the plains and force them to live on reservations, poor-quality lands unwanted by whites—at least not then. It was a brutal strategy, and Sheridan later admitted that the Indians' cause was just, his own people wrong: "We took away their country and their means of support, broke up their mode of living, their habits of life . . . introduced disease and decay among them. And it was for this and against this that they made war. Could anyone expect less?"[6] Still, war is war, and soldiers must do as they are told.

Not all Americans agreed with this strategy. The slaughter of the buffalo shocked many people. They thought it shameful to destroy so many innocent creatures for their skins alone. In Texas, lawmakers debated a bill to halt the killing immediately. Sheridan objected and rushed to Austin to explain why. Instead of stopping the hunters, he told the legislature, they should be given a medal for public service. One side of the medal would show a dead buffalo, the other a sad-faced Indian. "These men . . . are destroying the Indians' commissary; and it is a well-known fact that an army losing its base of supplies is placed at a great disadvantage. . . . [For] the sake of lasting peace, let them kill, skin, and sell until the buffaloes are exterminated. Then your prairies can be covered with speckled cattle and the festive cowboy, who follows the hunter as a . . . forerunner of an advanced civilization."[7] Sheridan made his point. The bill was defeated, and the slaughter continued unchecked.

Meantime, Sheridan's men prepared for action. The Indian-fighting army was a scaled-down version of the Union army. When the Civil War ended, most of the troops were discharged. Overnight a million-man force, the largest on earth, shrank to twenty-five thousand officers and men. Cutbacks forced nearly all officers to accept lower ranks or leave the service. Generals became colonels, colonels majors, majors captains, and so on down the line. Though this hurt their careers, it helped the army. For over a generation, every officer was a combat veteran of proven ability.

The men they led typified the American "melting pot." Irish, English, German, Italian, and Russian immigrants rubbed shoulders with those whose grandfathers had followed George Washington. And they were just as tough. As veterans used to say: "A trooper shouldn't never drown, get kicked to death, or die of some sickness—a trooper should *bleed*!" He must "die hard"; that is, die in battle.

Many had already shed their blood—and they looked it. Injuries that mean discharge from today's army were ignored back then. A soldier might limp badly or hobble on an artificial leg. There were one-armed and one-eyed soldiers. Men with missing fingers and toes, shot off or frozen off in long-ago campaigns, served in the Indian-fighting army. No one noticed their "handicap," or cared about them. Men could serve as long as they could fight.

The army also had its share of ex-Confederates and former slaves. After the Civil War, four black regiments—the Ninth and Tenth cavalries and the Twenty-fourth and Twenty-fifth infantries—were stationed on the Great Plains. Though enlisted men were black, their officers were white. White officers thought highly of their men and were proud to lead them. "They are good troops," said General Sherman. "They make first-rate sentinels, are faithful to their trust, and are as brave as the occasion calls for." Blacks had a lower desertion rate than whites and were usually in better physical condition. White settlers praised their courage during the Indian wars. So did the Indians, who called them "buffalo soldiers," because their hair resembled the coarse, knotted hair of the buffalo. Indians, too, were part of the Indian-fighting army. Certain tribes hated each other long before whites ever set foot on the plains. Becoming army scouts allowed them to settle scores and be paid for it by Uncle Sam.

The cavalry was the backbone of the frontier army. Caval-

Frederic Remington's sketch of an Apache Indian and a black "buffalo soldier" of the Tenth Cavalry Regiment in 1888.

rymen, like cowboys, were thin and wiry, with a top weight of 165 pounds. Their pay, however, was not nearly as good as the cowboys'. Privates earned $13 a month, rising to $16 after five years. Officers did better. Lieutenants, for example, received $125 a month, the same as trail bosses.

Cavalry units were based at a hundred forts scattered from Canada to Mexico. Most plains forts were not surrounded by walls of logs set in the ground and pointed at the top. They were of open construction, with rows of buildings arranged around a parade ground. Unmarried soldiers lived in barracks; families had quarters in "soapsuds row," where wives did the family washing. In addition, there were officers' quarters, headquarters, a hospital, guardhouse, blacksmith's shop, mess hall, and warehouses. A fort's real defense was its troops, not its fortifications. No Great Plains fort was ever captured by Indians.

Life at a fort took a lot of getting used to. Barracks, though roomier and neater than cowboy bunkhouses, were still quite primitive. Simple things, like bathtubs, were often lacking. One could spend a lifetime in the service without taking a bath. The soldier's day began with reveille at 5:30 A.M. and ended with taps at 10:00 P.M. During that time he stood for roll calls, cared

Fort Sill, Indian Territory, 1871. Unlike forts in the eastern woodlands, forts on the Great Plains were not surrounded by log walls. For defense, the buildings were arranged in a large square protected by artillery. No Great Plains fort was ever captured by Indians.

for his mount, did guard duty, and went on "fatigues," work details to dig wells, build roads, and string telegraph wire.

The cavalryman wore an oversize blue coat and baggy blue pants with a yellow stripe along each seam; that is why Indians called him "bluecoat" and "yellowlegs." In addition, he had a slouch hat, high boots, and a bandanna knotted around his neck. Despite movies and television, he did not use a sword in battle. The blade, three feet long and weighing five pounds, was no match for the Indian's fourteen-foot lance. The cavalryman's basic weapon, like the cowboy's, was the six-shooter. The Colt Army .44 was fourteen inches long and weighed three pounds. The extra length allowed him to pistol-whip an enemy when the gun was empty and there was no time to reload. A carbine, or short-barreled rifle, was used at longer ranges.

Soldiering on the plains required a special brand of courage. In "civilized" warfare, captives are put into prisoner-of-war camps. Life may be hard in these camps, but the enemy is bound to obey certain rules. Prisoners must be fed and the wounded given medical attention. Deliberately mistreating them, let alone killing them, is a serious crime. After the Civil War, the commander of Andersonville prison in Georgia was hung for mistreating Union captives.

It was different out west. "War is dreadful anyway," an officer's wife noted, "but an Indian war is worst of all. They respected no code of warfare, flags of truce. . . . It is like fighting to exterminate wild animals, horrible beasts." A soldier's daughter reported that Indians had no respect for the dead. She saw one victim with her own eyes: "Sargt. Williams of Co. 'G' got separated from the company and was shot in the head, stripped of his clothing, heart cut out, nose cut off, hacked and split and scalped with 16 arrows shot into his body."[8]

Williams was "lucky," because he died instantly. Captives, however, were tortured. Knowing this, soldiers were terrified of being taken alive. "As the volume of Indian fire seemed to increase," said a soldier, describing a battle, " 'No surrender' was the word passed around the thin skirmish line. Each of us would, if he found it necessary, have blown out his brains rather than fall alive into Indian hands."[9] A quick bullet was better than a lingering death.

Most terrifying was the thought of one's family undergoing torture. Army wives carried pocket derringers and knew how to use them. If capture seemed certain, they were prepared to shoot their children before turning the weapon on themselves. As a result, little mercy was shown by either side in the struggle for the Great Plains. Cavalrymen frequently shot wounded Indians to avenge lost comrades. Some soldiers repaid the enemy in kind: They took their scalps. State governments offered bounties for Indian scalps, as they did for wolf pelts.

Sheridan took the offensive after Adobe Walls. The Comanche and their allies were to be found, defeated, and sent to a reservation at Fort Sill, Indian Territory. There they would learn the white man's ways. They would be taught his religion and to earn their living as he did, by farming. Never again would they be allowed to roam freely on the plains.

That was easier said than done. Comanche hit-and-run tactics were as deadly as ever; indeed, they had improved their methods since their battles with the Texas Rangers forty years earlier. Whenever a war party moved, scouts patrolled ten miles in every direction, making surprise impossible. This forced the cavalry to fight on the Indians' terms or not at all. If the Indians didn't like the way things were going, they broke contact and sped away. But Comanche in retreat could be as dangerous as Comanche on the attack. As they fled, they often left decoys to draw their pursuers into ambush.

B-67

Sheridan had to pin down the enemy long enough to fight him. But how? The answer lay in one word: winter. Winter deprived the enemy of his chief advantage, his mobility. Plains Indians had to prepare for winter months in advance. By midfall, after the last big buffalo hunt, they gathered in large encampments. There the women made pemmican, sewed warm clothing, and readied their tepees for cold weather. When winter arrived, north winds sent the plains into a deep freeze. Cold and snow made it difficult to move about for long periods of time. Quick getaways were impossible.

The cavalry, however, were all-weather soldiers. Railroad trains could keep field units supplied year-round. Sheridan planned to strike when the Indians were least able to defend

The Civil War hero General Philip Sheridan believed that it was necessary to exterminate the buffalo in order to break the power of the Plains Indian tribes.

themselves. He would find their encampments, destroy their winter stores, and force them onto the open plains. Cold, hunger, and exposure would do the rest.

Late in the summer of 1874, cavalry units set out from Colorado, Kansas, Indian Territory, New Mexico, and Texas. Entering the Texas panhandle from five directions, they crisscrossed it again and again, searching for the main Comanche encampment. Troopers rode from sunrise to sunset, eating dust every mile of the way. As they rode, they sang a song, a true description of army life:

> There was sergeant John McCaffery
> and Captain Donahue,
> Oh, they made us march and toe the mark
> in gallant Company Q.
> Oh, the drums would roll. Upon by soul,
> this is the style we'd go,
> Forty miles a day on beans and hay
> in the Regular Army, O!

One of the units was led by Colonel Ranald S. Mackenzie. Mackenzie, known to the Indians as Bad Hand (thanks to a Civil War wound), was a brilliant officer. On September 27, his Fourth Cavalry met a party of Comanchero with wagons full of trade goods. The Comanchero were of mixed Mexican and Indian parentage. Based in New Mexico, they gave the Comanche guns and ammunition in exchange for horses and loot. Occasionally, they accepted white prisoners, forcing their relatives to buy their freedom or see them returned to the Comanche.

José Tafoya, the group's leader, knew the location of Quanah Parker's camp. After some hard-fisted "persuasion," he was glad to tell all. The Comanche were in Palo Duro Canyon, a huge gash in the earth near the present city of Amarillo. Carved by a branch of the Red River, it is eight hundred feet deep and three to five miles wide at the bottom. The surrounding land is so flat that the canyon is invisible until you are right at the rim. No white man had ever seen it—until then.

Mackenzie sent a sergeant and two Indian scouts to pinpoint the enemy's location. Moving cautiously, they left their horses

Colonel Ranald "Bad Hand" Mackenzie broke the power of the Comanche by attacking their encampment in the Palo Duro Canyon and killing nearly all of their horses. This picture was taken in 1886; Mackenzie died insane three years later.

at a safe distance and crawled to the edge of the Palo Duro. Peering over, they were amazed at the sight. There, spread out on the canyon floor, were hundreds of tepees. Nearby, grazing peacefully, were more horses than they could count. Not only had they found the main Comanche camp, but that of their Kiowa and Southern Cheyenne allies.

The Fourth Cavalry arrived the next morning. Mackenzie looked over the edge and noticed a steep path winding its way to the canyon floor. Without hesitating, he ordered his men to dismount and go down single file, leading their horses by the bridle. They were undetected—most of the way—since the Indians felt so safe that they had posted only one lookout. The soldiers were still on the path when the lookout saw them and gave a war whoop. A bullet silenced him but alerted the camp.

It was too late. Troopers were already taking positions between the camp and the horse herd. Rather than be trapped, women and children fled upstream, then up another trail to the plain above. Braves fired from behind boulders to cover their escape, then made their own getaway. Indian casualties in the "battle" were four killed and perhaps twice as many wounded; one cavalryman was slightly wounded. Even so, Bad Hand Mackenzie had won a stunning victory.

The Indians escaped with little more than their lives. Left behind was a winter's supply of food, buffalo robes, clothing, tepee covers, and other precious items. These were burned. More important, 1,424 horses were captured. "Shoot them," Mackenzie snapped. Their sun-bleached bones would be a Texas landmark for generations.

The southern Plains tribes had come full circle. Once again they were on foot. Although they might avoid the cavalry, there was no avoiding the winter, which came early in 1874.

In this old print, U.S. Cavalrymen have rounded up cold, starving Indians and are leading them to captivity.

Cold and exhausted, they wandered the windswept plains, searching for shelter and food. When their moccasins wore out, they went barefoot, leaving bloody tracks in the snow. Now and then they killed some buffalo, strays overlooked by the white hunters. A new song was heard among these proud warrior people. It was a plea for mercy to Wakan Taka:

> Father, have pity on me,
> Father, have pity on me.
> I am crying for thirst,
> I am crying for thirst.
> All is gone—I have nothing to eat.
> All is gone—I have nothing to eat.

Gradually, they turned themselves in at Fort Sill. Lone Wolf and his Kiowa came first, in February 1875. The Southern Cheyenne arrived several weeks later, along with bands of Comanche. Only Quanah Parker's Quahadi remained outside. They held out until spring, the last Comanche and the last southern Plains tribes to surrender. Quanah now championed peace with the same skill and energy as he had once followed the warpath. In the years that followed, he worked to create goodwill among his people and their conquerors. He died in 1911, honored and respected by both races.

With the buffalo gone and the red man defeated, nothing barred the Western Trail. Dodge City saw its first longhorns in 1876. That same year Charles Goodnight drove eighteen hundred head of cattle into the Palo Duro. In time his JA Ranch would graze a hundred thousand cattle on a million acres of prime land. The future, as General Sheridan predicted, belonged to the "speckled cattle and the festive cowboy."

The great buffalo hunt moved north.

The North was controlled by the largest of the Plains tribes. The Chippewa, old enemies, knew them as *nadowe-is-iw*— "rattlesnake." French-Canadian traders who met them in the 1700s shortened it to Sioux. The Americans later adopted that name, which they pronounced "Soo." Tribesmen, however, called themselves *dah-kota*, or "alliance of friends." Part of their homeland later became the states of North and South Dakota.

Captain William J. Fetterman, who rode
his patrol into a Sioux trap

The Sioux once ruled from the headwaters of the Mississippi in Minnesota to the banks of the Yellowstone and Powder rivers in Montana and Wyoming. Everyone, red and white, knew their reputation as warriors. Fighting them, a U.S. Army doctor explained, was a shortcut to the next world. It was plain "Siouxicidal."

The Oglala Sioux, a branch of the Dakota nation, guarded the Powder River country. Lying between the Black Hills and Big Horn Mountains of South Dakota and Wyoming, this was a special place, a blessed place. It had everything. Vast herds of buffalo grazed there. Streams of melted snow poured from the Big Horns, watering the tree-covered valleys. The Great Spirit smiled upon the land.

That began to change after the Civil War. As on the southern plains, railroads probed westward into the buffalo country. Locomotives ("bad medicine wagons") belched coal smoke into the clear air. Trains brought hunters, followed by settlers. To protect them, the army built "war houses"—forts—at key points. The Oglala had no choice but to call upon their cousins, the Hunkpapa and Miniconjou, to help defend their tribal lands.

For two years, the Sioux attacked trains, killed settlers, and ambushed army patrols. One patrol—eighty-one troopers led by Captain William J. Fetterman—rode into a trap and was annihilated. Finally, in April 1868, the whites decided to make peace. Leaders of the Sioux and Northern Cheyenne were invited to a council at Fort Laramie, Wyoming. A treaty was signed in which the government abandoned three forts and closed the area to whites "as long as the grass grows and water runs." The Indians promised to live in peace with the United States and to allow the railroads to build across their lands.

The Fort Laramie Treaty was too good to be true. In the early 1870s, rumors told of gold in the Black Hills. Indians called gold the "crazy-making metal," for the very word made whites crazy with greed. They would go anywhere, do anything, to find gold. Treaty or no treaty, prospectors invaded the forbidden area.

The Black Hills were sacred. They were *Paha Sapa*, the center of the world, where Sioux warriors went to speak to Wakan Taka. The fact that the land was sacred and that whites had no right to it did not concern gold seekers. They came singly or

in small groups. And the Sioux killed them singly or in small groups. But there were always others to take their place.

The government decided to act before things got out of hand. In the summer of 1874, an expedition led by George Armstrong Custer was sent to learn the truth about the Black Hills. Custer's report confirmed the rumors. Not only was there gold, but deep veins of it laced the hillsides. Prospectors went wild at the news. They swarmed into the Black Hills by the thousands. Mining camps sprang up at Deadwood, Gold River Gulch, and Homestake. Within fifty years, $250 million worth of gold was taken from the Black Hills mines.

Washington could see a massacre coming. Its solution was simple: buy the Black Hills and send the Indians to reservations. The Sioux were astonished. The very idea of selling holy ground

Members of the federal government meet with Sioux leaders at Fort Laramie, Wyoming, and agree to give up their forts and close the area to whites. This treaty, like all others, was soon broken.

insulted their religion. Not a twig. Not a stone. Not a blade of grass. Nothing was for sale. Anyone who violated Paha Sapa would indeed pay a price—in blood. Oglala braves let government agents know this in no uncertain terms. They circled them on horseback, firing rifles into the air and chanting:

> The Black Hills is my land and I love it,
> And whoever interferes
> Will hear this gun.

Washington got tough. The Sioux were given an offer they dared not refuse. Either they surrender the Black Hills peacefully or the army would take them by force. This was robbery, but it had all happened before, many times, and would happen again. Since 1789, the United States has made 370 Indian treaties and has broken every one of them. The Fort Laramie Treaty was no exception.

In the spring of 1876, the Sioux prepared for a showdown. Their main bands, the Oglala and Hunkpapa, were led by men

The Homestake Mine was one of the first to take gold from the Black Hills.

Known to whites as Sitting Bull, Tatanka Iyotake was the leading chief and medicine man of the Hunkpapa Sioux.

of genius. The Hunkpapa chief was Tatanka Iyotake, better known as Sitting Bull. Born about 1831, Sitting Bull was recognized throughout the northern plains as a warrior and holy man. A natural leader, he had a gift for getting people to work together. The Oglala chief was Tashunca-uitco, or Crazy Horse. But there was nothing crazy about Crazy Horse, who was born about 1842. His name means "untamed horse," rather than "insane horse." Crazy Horse was as spirited as a young mustang and as disciplined as an Olympic athlete. All agreed that he was the bravest of the brave. First to attack and last to retreat, he inspired others with his courage.

The Sioux gathered at a camp along the Little Bighorn River in southern Montana. General Sheridan, learning of their whereabouts, planned to "bag" them in one swift move. A cavalry force was to come down the valley of the Little Bighorn from the north. At the same time, a second force would come up the valley from the south. When in position, they would attack together, catching the enemy in a crossfire. It was a fine plan, except for one weakness. The southern force, the Seventh Cavalry, was led by George Armstrong Custer.

Custer was born in Ohio in 1839. A poor student, he graduated from the United States Military Academy in West Point, New York, at the bottom of his class in 1861. But low grades did not matter during the Civil War. What mattered was ability, courage, and luck. And Custer had these in abundance. Within three years, he rose from second lieutenant to major general of cavalry. No wonder comrades called him the Boy General. When the war ended, he accepted the rank of colonel in order to stay in the army.

Custer was a six-footer with blue eyes and golden brown hair that reached down to his shoulders. Cavalrymen called him Old Curly. Indians called him Long Hair the Woman Killer, because his men had killed women and children during a raid on a Cheyenne village. Custer, in his own eyes, knew everything and could do anything. "I'll show 'em," he told General Sheridan. "The Seventh can lick any force the Indians can throw into the field, all the Indians on the plains, if necessary."[10]

Old Curly reached the Little Bighorn on June 25, 1876. The centennial of the Declaration of Independence was just nine days away, and he meant to give the nation a birthday present to remember.

No sooner had Custer arrived than he disobeyed orders. Instead of waiting for the northern force, he attacked alone. With fewer than six hundred men, he divided his force into thirds and charged the sprawling camp. Though taken by surprise, the

Men of the Open Range by Charles M. Russell
(Montana State Historical Society, McKay Collection)

The Great West, lithograph by Currier & Ives
(The Metropolitan Museum of Art; gift of George S. Amory in memory of Renee Carhart Amory, 1966)

Lieutenant Colonel George Armstrong Custer and five troops of the Seventh Cavalry Regiment were annihilated by the Sioux and Cheyenne when they tried to attack an Indian encampment on the Little Bighorn River on June 25, 1876.

Sioux rallied. At the first sign of trouble, Crazy Horse leaped onto his horse. Naked except for a cloth around his waist, he rode toward the advancing cavalry. "*Hookahey! Hookahey* Dakotas!" he cried. "It is a good day to fight! It is a good day to die! Stout hearts, brave hearts, to the front! Weak hearts and cowards to the rear!"

No Indian turned back. Instead, two thousand braves swept forward. Within minutes, they broke the attack and sent the cavalry fleeing for their lives. Custer and 225 men were cornered on a barren hillside overlooking the Little Bighorn. The troopers fought desperately, trying to make every shot count. Some killed their horses and took cover behind the bleeding carcasses. But

➤➤➤ *151*

it was no use. As their defenses crumbled, men shot themselves rather than be taken alive. Their colonel was among the last to die, felled by a hail of bullets. The Indians then combed the hillside, killing the wounded, taking scalps, and stripping the bodies. They had wiped out the enemy at a cost of thirty-two killed.

"Vengeance!" cried newspaper headlines. And vengeance it would be. Throughout the summer, reinforcements and supplies poured into the plains forts. Ranald Mackenzie and the Fourth Cavalry rode up from Texas. Weaving his forces into a giant net, Sheridan set out to destroy the Sioux and their Northern Cheyenne allies.

It was the Palo Duro all over again, only on a larger scale. The Indians were hunted without letup and attacked without mercy. They were defeated at War Bonnet Creek, Slim Buttes, Crazy Woman Fork, Tongue River, and a dozen other places. Crazy Horse surrendered, only to be murdered by soldiers. Sitting Bull led his people to safety in Canada. Returning in 1881, he was eventually killed by Indian police at Standing Rock Reservation, South Dakota.

By 1877, the northern plains, like the southern plains, were quiet. The Indians were imprisoned on reservations, living on handouts of government beef. Those who ventured onto the plains did so at their peril. Anyone who "jumped" the reservation could be shot on sight.

Settlers once told of seeing a group of Indians approaching on foot. Drawing their guns, they prepared for battle. But there was no need to worry. As the braves came closer, they saw them carrying a long banner. They were led by Spotted Tail, a celebrated war chief. The banner read SPOTTED TAIL AND HIS BAND OF FRIENDLY SIOUX. Even these brave men went in fear.

The defeat of the Sioux made the northern plains safe for buffalo hunters. As a result, the last herds, millions of animals, were exterminated within six years. By 1883, fewer than eleven hundred buffalo survived on the Great Plains. These were saved in the nick of time by the U.S. government. Hunting was finally outlawed, and the remaining animals were placed on Montana's National Buffalo Range and in Yellowstone National Park. By

the early 1900s, the buffalo was no longer in danger of extinction. But, like the Indian, it could not leave its "reservations."

The Indian and the buffalo were to be united one last time. In 1913 the U.S. Treasury Department issued a five-cent coin with a portrait of an Indian on one side and a buffalo on the other. It was meant as a tribute to the first Americans. But red men saw it differently. "What a bad joke," said an elderly brave upon seeing the shiny coin. General Sheridan, though long dead, had the last word.

Sitting Bull, shown here with members of his family, spent his last days at Standing Rock reservation.

➤➤➤ 153

CHAPTER SIX

Empire of Grass

"I believe I would know an old cowboy in hell with his hide burnt off. It's the way they stand and walk and talk. . . . Only a few of us are left now and they are scattered from Texas to Canada. The rest have left the wagon and gone ahead across the big divide, looking for a new range. I hope they find good water and plenty of grass. But wherever they are is where I want to go."

—*Teddy Blue Abbott*, We Pointed Them North

CAVALRY PATROLS ROUTINELY LEFT FORT LARAMIE DURING THE late 1800s. There were always settlers to escort, a band of Indians to investigate, or a railroad work crew to help out of a tight spot. If the soldiers traveled eastward in a straight line, toward central Nebraska, they might notice something odd. The grass to their right was short, clumpy, buffalo grass. It was the same to their left, except for a scattering of taller grasses, like bluestem and needle-and-thread. This is no accident. Scientists tell us that they were following the natural boundary of the southern and northern plains.

These areas differ in several important ways. The southern plains, hot in summer and cold in winter, are open, flat, and covered with short grasses. The northern plains are broken by

A typical northern plains ranch
in Montana.

canyons and buttes, isolated hills with flat tops rising sharply from the surrounding countryside. Summers there are cooler and shorter, winters colder and longer, than in the south.

The farther north you go, the more tall grasses you find. In the fall, these become dry and turn yellow. But they remain nutritious the winter long, though buried by blizzards. Snow could not deprive buffalo or antelope of a hardy meal. They survived the severest winters by pawing or poking their snouts through the snow to get at the grass. Cattle, however, do not feed in this way. If grass is not visible, they will not dig through snow to reach it. They will wander about, bawl, grow weaker— and starve. For this reason ranching was thought to be impossible on the northern plains.

Freight companies hauling supplies to Fort Laramie learned differently. About the year 1859, blizzards caught a number of wagon trains in the open. Unable to go forward, the drivers decided to spend the winter in the fort. But since there was no room for their oxen, they turned them loose to freeze or starve. When spring came, however, they found the oxen not only alive, but fat and healthy. The reason is quite simple. Not even the worst blizzard will cover all grass all the time. High winds cause the snow to drift, uncovering large patches of it.

That discovery opened the cattleman's last frontier. Beginning in 1879, herds of Texas longhorns passed through Dodge City, bound for Nebraska and the Dakotas. Other herds went by way of New Mexico, heading for Wyoming and Montana. Their way was often blocked by buffalo, which cowboys had to scare off the trail, at no small risk to themselves. But by the fall of 1883, the buffalo were gone, and the Sioux imprisoned on reservations. Millions of acres of grassland—an empire of grass—were just waiting to be claimed.

Texans brought their cattle and their skills northward. In the early days, northern cowboys were nearly always Texans. The work was familiar, at least during part of the year. There were still two roundups, though trail drives were shorter. Railroads were only a few days away, not months away as in the Long Drive from Texas to Kansas. The North had no towns like Abilene or Dodge City, and celebrations at the end of a trail were pretty tame.

The main difference was in the winter work. Winters were harsher than in Texas. A cowboy had to be out and about on the coldest days. Dressed in a woolen parka, his hat pulled down over his ears, he drove cattle to places where the wind

Members of a ranch family pose near their house, made from bricks of prairie sod.

had cleared snow from the grass. He cut ice to open water holes, hauled firewood, and rescued weak calves. To help with this task, he had two "winter horses," strong mounts that could carry him while he held a calf in his arms. In addition, he had to shoot wolves and eagles. Wolf packs became bold during the winter, attacking even the strongest bulls; eagles liked nothing better than a tender calf.

Winter took a lot of getting used to. On clear days, the reflection of sun on snow could make you temporarily blind. There were no sunglasses back then; all you could do was paint your cheekbones with charcoal to reduce the glare. Men's faces became badly sunburned, their skin and lips cracking from the frost. But it was the cold that really wore them out. Cowboys came down with consumption (tuberculosis) from exposure to the cold; cold and damp also caused rheumatism. Many Texans gave up and returned home after a season or two in the North. One fellow, whose name we do not know, expressed himself in a song:

> Oh, I am a Texas cowboy
> Far away from home,
> If ever I get back to Texas
> I never more will roam.
>
> Montana is too cold for me
> And the winters are too long;
> Before the roundups do begin
> Our money is all gone.
>
> All along the Yellowstone
> 'Tis cold the year around;
> You will surely get consumption
> By sleeping on the ground.

Nevertheless, ranching flourished. America was prosperous, and its cities demanded beef as never before. In 1879 longhorns sold for between $7.00 and $8.00 a head, a record high. But that was just the beginning. The same cow brought $9.50 in 1880, $12.00 in 1881, and $35.00 in 1882. It seemed that the sky was the limit.

It was at this point that the railroads stepped into the picture. The government, we recall, had given them millions of acres of land to encourage building after the Civil War. Yet that land was worthless in itself. The railroads could only make large profits by selling it and then charging settlers to use their services.

The high price of cattle was just what the railroads needed. To stimulate interest in the northern plains, the railroads paid newspaper reporters to plant stories about easy money in ranching. James S. Brisbin, a retired general, helped with a book, *The Beef Bonanza; or, How to Get Rich on the Plains.* Brisbin, who knew little about cattle, showed how to turn grass into gold. He "proved" that one could earn a 50 percent profit each year, every year, over and above expenses. Getting rich was as easy as writing numbers on a slip of paper.

People rushed to cash in on the bonanza. Eastern businessmen, knowing even less about cattle than Brisbin, poured millions into the northern plains. Railroad lands were purchased at top prices. Branch lines were built. Giant cattle companies were formed, ranches laid out, and longhorns brought from Texas. Wealthy foreigners, seeing a good thing, also reached into their pockets. While most hired professional managers, a few went west to look after their interests in person.

Among them was the Marquis de Mores, a French nobleman. In 1883 the marquis arrived at the town of Little Missouri, North Dakota. Greed—at least greed for money—may not have been his only reason for coming so far. Rumor said that he had royal blood, and that he hoped to use the fortune gained from ranching to overthrow the French government and crown himself king.

Whatever his reasons, the marquis did things in a big way. No sooner had he arrived than he bought land and built his own town, Medora, named after his wife, the daughter of a New York banker. To keep her from getting homesick, he built a twenty-eight-room mansion and furnished it with expensive European furniture. The mansion had a complete staff: butler, coachman, gardener, laundress, chambermaids, and cooks. Their child's nursery was filled with toys.

The marquis invested millions, mainly his father-in-law's money, in ranch and packing plants. He planned to create a

Among Theodore Roosevelt's neighbors in the Dakota Badlands were the French-born Marquis de Mores and his wife, Medora von Hoffman, daughter of a New York banker. The marquis hoped to make a fortune in the cattle industry and use the profits to make himself ruler of France.

vast business, every part of which he controlled from his mansion. He would slaughter his own cattle in his own slaughterhouses, process the meat in his own plants, and send it to market in his own refrigerated railcars. By shipping just the meat, rather than the entire animal, he would save on freight costs and increase profits. It was a clever scheme, but too far ahead of its time. He lost millions of dollars and returned to France in 1887. After further ventures in China and India, he died fighting Arabs in North Africa.

The marquis's neighbor was a young man named Theodore Roosevelt. Born in 1858, Roosevelt was destined to be one of the giants of American history. Theodore—he hated the nickname Teddy—had been a sickly child with poor vision. Fearing for his life, his wealthy father built a gymnasium at home and hired an athletic coach. The boy ran, did push-ups, and worked out on parallel bars for hours each day. But boxing was his best sport, and while a student at Harvard University he became

A formal portrait of Medora von Hoffman. Her husband, the Marquis de Mores, named the town of Medora after her.

school champion. Upon graduation, he returned home, became a lawyer, and married. Life seemed perfect until his mother and wife died on the same day. TR, as his friends called him, was heartbroken. To pull himself together, in 1883 he went west and bought the Maltese Cross Ranch.

Cowboys did not know what to make of this stranger. They had seen other dudes but never the likes of him. To begin with,

Theodore Roosevelt as a rancher. This "dude," with his eastern accent and thick eyeglasses, won cowboys' respect through hard work and ability with his fists.

he wore eyeglasses, rare things in the West at that time. His thick glasses earned him the nickname Four Eyes. Another nickname was Toothadore, because of his large teeth and odd way of laughing. He'd laugh by setting his jaws, baring his teeth, and letting go with an explosive "Hah!" If he really liked something, he'd cry "Bully!" or "By Godfrey, this is fun!" On his first roundup, he called in his Harvard accent: "Hasten forward quickly there!" Everyone who heard him burst out laughing. It became a ranch joke, and for weeks afterward cowboys ordered one another about with "Hasten forward quickly there!"

Roosevelt, however, was not merely an adventure-seeking dude. When he did something, it was with all his energy. He did not expect cowboys to respect him because he was the boss. Respect, he knew, must be earned. And he earned theirs by becoming one of them. He asked their advice, learned their ways, and worked as hard as any hired hand. But it was his talent for "fisticuffs" that won their hearts.

One night, a bully crossed his path in a hotel saloon. "Four Eyes is going to treat," he announced, drawing a six-shooter. Again and again he repeated the taunt. Roosevelt put up with this for a few minutes, then lost patience. "Well, if I've got to, I've got to," he muttered, rising from his table. Whereupon he flattened the bully with a punch in the jaw. It was a blow worthy of Bear River Smith, and the cowboys knew it. They changed his nickname from Four Eyes to Old Four Eyes; it was an honor to be known as "old." TR had become one of them, a man among men.[1]

Roosevelt returned to the East in 1886 to follow a career in politics. Yet he never forgot his years in North Dakota or the friends he made there. When the Spanish-American War began in 1898, he became colonel of a volunteer cavalry regiment. Known as the Rough Riders, the regiment was made up of two types of recruits. There were wealthy, educated easterners eager to fight for their country. The bulk of the regiment, however, were westerners with names like Cherokee Bill, Dead Shot Jim, Lariat Ned, Rattlesnake Pete, and Prayerful James. The regiment boasted eight lawmen, including Marshal Ben Daniels of Dodge City, and an unreported number of outlaws. One, Charlie Younger, was the son of Bob Younger of the Jesse James gang. Most of the Rough Riders were bowlegged, and all were more comfortable on horseback than walking.

Roosevelt returned from the war a national hero. Elected governor of New York, he soon became the Republican party's candidate for vice president. Sometimes, while campaigning out West, TR ran into hostile audiences. But he did not scare easily. He once asked a friend named Seth, a retired gunfighter, to sit behind him on the speaker's platform. Lo and behold, the audience behaved perfectly. Seth had let it be known that he would "plug" anyone who interrupted.[2]

Roosevelt won the election but was vice president for only a short time. When President William McKinley was assassinated in 1901, TR became the twenty-sixth president of the United States. Opponents were astonished. "That damned cowboy,"

As president, Theodore Roosevelt helped save the buffalo and added to our national parks system.

they growled, was unfit to live in the White House. Cowboys were, in fact, always welcome there—guns and all. TR once asked a visitor not to shoot at the feet of the British ambassador, a stuffy gentleman who couldn't take a "joke." A special favorite was Bat Masterson, who had become sports editor for a New York newspaper. The president admired the old lawman, and they exchanged many letters. Roosevelt loved the West and vowed to preserve as much of it as possible. During his presidency, millions of acres were added to the national parks system and efforts made to protect wildlife. Americans owe a lot to their "cowboy president."

Even as TR worked on his ranch, he saw that times were changing. The year he started was one of drought on the Great Plains. Weeks passed without a drop of rain. Water holes and streams became dust bowls. As grass dried to straw, prairie fires broke out, sending plumes of smoke thousands of feet into the sky. Without water, cowboys had to find other ways to prevent fire from spreading. Sometimes they would shoot a longhorn, split it in half along the backbone, and drag it along the fire's edge, using the blood to stop the fire. Ranchers, facing bankruptcy, begged Mother Nature for mercy:

Prairie fires, won't you please stop?
Let thunder roll and water drop;
It frightens me to see the smoke—
Unless it's stopped I'll go dead broke.

Owners of large ranches could read the handwriting on the wall. Clearly, the era of the open range was closing. In the future a rancher, to survive, would have to control all the grass and water he could get. The wealthy began to buy or rent more grazing land, plus the right to use water on others' property. And if that was not enough, they turned their cattle loose on government lands. They had no legal right to these lands, but so long as no one claimed them, they saw no reason to let the grass go to waste.

They were aided by barbed wire, a recent invention. Building fences had always been difficult on the Great Plains. Wooden railing, brought by train, cost many times more than the land itself. Although stone might be found locally, it was scarce, and fencing even a small area required weeks of backbreaking labor. Joseph F. Glidden, an Illinois farmer, solved their problem when his wife asked for a fence to keep dogs out of her garden. Glidden bought two strands of wire from the local hardware store. One strand he kept long. The other he cut into small pieces, pointed at the ends, which he twisted around the long strand. He then cut this into sections and nailed the pieces at different levels to posts set in the ground. Dogs never bothered Mrs. G's garden again.

Glidden patented his invention and opened a factory in De Kalb, Illinois. In 1874, his first year in business, he sold 10,000 pounds of barbed wire. Demand soared. Each year thereafter, he sold several times more than the year before: 600,000 pounds in 1875; 26,655,000 pounds in 1878; and 80,500,000 pounds in 1880. He had found the ideal fence. Cheap and easy to build, it took up little space, withstood high winds, and did not cause snowdrifts. Yet there was another advantage, which Glidden had not foreseen. Barbed wire was as effective on people as on animals. Before long, the world's armies were buying it to strengthen fortifications and for use on the battlefield.

Wealthy ranchers saw barbed wire as a way to get "free" acres of grazing land for their herds. They began by stringing fences around small ranches and farms. Public lands were enclosed for private use. Fences blocked roads and slowed mail delivery. Schools and churches became islands surrounded by wire.

Fences were a matter of life and death to the small landowner. A rancher cut off from grass and water could not stay in business. A farmer completely surrounded by other farmers' land could not go to town for supplies or bring his crops to market. No wonder they hated everything to do with "bob wahr." Its inventor, they said, should have it wound around him in a ball and the ball rolled into hell. Barbed wire, to be sure, came from the devil. As one song put it:

> They say that heaven is a free range land,
> Good-bye, good-bye, O fare you well;
> But it's barbed wire fence for the devil's hat band;
> And barbed wire blankets down in hell.

Opponents of fencing wrote letters to state lawmakers. But when their letters were ignored, they acted on their own. Armed bands called Blue Devils and Owls began to cut fences at night. Their work done, they left a warning about rebuilding: a picture of a coffin or a hangman's noose dangling from a fence post. Fence cutters were prepared to kill for the open range.

Wealthy ranchers were prepared to kill for their fences. On dark, moonless nights, they waited for the fence cutters to appear. Shots were exchanged. Men died. In Texas, shoot-outs were serious enough to be called the Fence Cutter Wars. At last, laws were passed making fence cutting punishable by five years in prison. At the same time, illegal fences were to be torn down and gates set every three miles in fences along public roads. The law, enforced by the Texas Rangers, was obeyed to the letter.

Waiting for a Chinook by Charles M. Russell
(Buffalo Bill Historical Center, Cody, Wyoming)

Custer's Last Stand by Edgar S. Paxton
(Buffalo Bill Historical Center, Cody, Wyoming)

Meantime, rising prices for beef led to overstocking, grazing more cattle than the land could support. This had not been a problem when the buffalo roamed the plains. Buffalo herds would eat the grass, drop their chips, and move on to fresh pasture. Their manure fertilized the soil and their hooves broke the ground, letting in air and moisture. Cattle are different. They bite off the grass at ground level, then eat the new shoots, never giving the grass a chance to recover. Eventually, the grass becomes thinner, allowing plants like thistle and tumbleweed to take over. When that happens, moisture runs off, the soil hardens, and the land turns to desert. Overstocking set the stage for ecological disaster.

The crisis came in 1886. That year was one of the hottest and driest ever seen on the Great Plains. The Southwest shimmered under the blazing sun for weeks. Temperatures soared past 100 degrees Fahrenheit and stayed there; often it was 115 in the shade. Texans tried to smile through their troubles. It was so hot, they joked, that potatoes came out of the ground cooked and ready to eat. It was so dry that fish in the streams

Taking the law into their own hands. Homesteaders in Custer County, Nebraska, cut barbed-wire fences erected by cattlemen to enclose their ranches and protect their water supplies.

were carrying toadstools as parasols. Even the cactus were heard to complain.

Smiles, however, could not change reality. By July, wells and water holes were bone-dry. Overstocked fields turned to dust and blew away in the wind. Dust fine as talcum powder came through doors and windows; people tasted it in their food, and when they closed their mouths, it crackled between their teeth. Cattle, crazed by thirst, went blind and died in droves. Prairie fires burned out of control, lighting the horizon as if the end of the world were near. Families, unable to earn a living, left the land. A sign nailed across a cabin door told of their despair:

250 MILES TO THE NEAREST POST OFFICE

100 MILES TO WOOD

20 MILES TO WATER

6 INCHES TO HELL

GOD BLESS OUR HOME

GONE TO LIVE WITH THE WIFE'S FOLKS

And on reservations Indians shook their heads knowingly. Wakan Taka *was* just. Surely, he was punishing the whites for what they had done to them and to the buffalo. Little did they know that the worst was still to come.

It was a glorious autumn, mild, clear, and sunny. At last the rains fell, reviving land and people. Old-timers, however, began to notice worrisome things. In Montana, along the upper reaches of the Missouri, migrating birds flew south early. Beaver and elk grew heavier coats than usual. White arctic owls appeared for the first time. Wakan Taka was preparing the winter of winters.

Snow fell on November 16. Though it fell on and off for the next ten weeks, it was nothing unusual and did not interfere with the Christmas or New Year's festivities. Then it happened. On January 28, the worst blizzard in history rolled across the plains from Canada to Texas. The sky turned black. Temperatures plummeted to sixty-eight degrees Fahrenheit below zero, while winds howled at sixty miles an hour. And it snowed. Lord, how it snowed! For three days and nights, snow fell at better than an inch an hour. Rancher John J. Callison remembered it well:

Only those who have experienced the terrors of a genuine blizzard can comprehend what it means and even then they cannot describe it in anything like adequate language. . . . [The] storm breaks with surprising suddenness. All at once the whole atmosphere becomes a whirling, seething mass of white, biting particles of icy snow that cut the skin like a set of sharp revolving blades. No living creature can face such an ordeal and live. Instinctively and from absolute necessity one turns his face down the wind, for breathing is impossible in any other position. Driven by the terrific onrushing blasts, the icy particles strike and sting like a thousand whips. The heaviest clothing does not protect the body and soon it becomes thoroughly chilled, as though it were suddenly plunged into a bath of ice water. The air itself becomes freezing cold. The whole world seems blotted out of existence. The eye can see nothing with distinctness—only a glittering whirl of dancing ice particles, that strike at one like frenzied demons. All sense of direction is lost. The mountain, the hills, the ridges, the valleys, have all disappeared. Only at one's feet can he see a bit of earth, and he is not quite sure of that. . . . Under such conditions a man is no better off than the poor dumb cattle.[3]

Going outdoors meant risking your life. Ravines filled with snow to a depth of a hundred feet, becoming level with the surrounding area. Horsemen, blinded by swirling snow, rode over the edge and were buried alive with their mounts. Farmers, struggling to go from house to barn, lost their way and wandered about until they died of exposure; some were found only a few feet from their doorsteps. A drunken cowboy left a saloon and froze stiff at the crossroads. Since the ground was too hard to dig a grave, friends stood him up and hung a lantern on him to help others find their way. There was not even safety behind "solid" walls. The wind blew through every crack, turning houses into icy tombs. Families were often found in one bed, huddled together in death.

Cattle were helpless in the open. They stood covered with snow, eyes frozen shut, icicles dangling from their muzzles. They crowded into ravines for shelter, only to be buried in snowslides. They starved, even though grass lay beneath the snow. Unable to help themselves, they gathered around ranch houses, bawling pitifully. But their owners had nothing for them. In Medora, cattle poisoned themselves by eating tar paper off the sides of cabins. Herds drifted southward before the wind, only to pile up against barbed-wire fences, where they froze. In the spring, streams of melting snow washed thousands of carcasses into the Missouri and its tributaries. Smaller streams, dammed by carcasses, backed up for miles. Only wolves were sleek and fat.

The "die-up," as it is still called, was a disaster. There had never been a spring roundup like that of 1887. It was a gloomy time, a time of fear and uncertainty. Instead of healthy animals, cowmen saw four-legged bags of bones. Ranchers lost between 40 and 90 percent of their livestock. Hundreds of small outfits were wiped out completely. Even big companies, many owned by eastern and European investors, went bankrupt. Yet the survivors had learned their lesson. Granville Stuart, who had introduced the longhorn into Montana, made a vow: "I never wanted to own again an animal that I couldn't feed or shelter."

After the die-up, ranchers turned to smaller herds of high-grade stock imported from England. These animals had short horns, short legs, and produced more meat. The days of the longhorn were numbered. When the last herds went to market, they were not replaced. A few have been kept as curiosities, but they are now scarcer than the buffalo.

High-grade stock had to be cared for in all seasons. You could afford to lose a $35 longhorn; you couldn't lose many $1,000 bulls and stay in business. To protect against the cold, barns were built throughout the Great Plains. More land—either purchased or rented—was fenced with barbed wire. The range was cut up into pasture or hayfields for growing winter feed. Water became less of a problem in the 1890s. Holes, called "tanks," were dug to collect rainwater and store it until needed. Iron-frame windmills were an inexpensive way of pumping water from deep wells. Veterinarians tended to the animals' health on a regular basis. Colleges were set up to teach modern methods of stock raising and farming. Ranching was no longer an adventure but a business and a science.

The railroad that took the ranchers' cattle to market proved to be a mixed blessing. During the Civil War, Congress had

passed the Homestead Act. Under this law any head of a household, male or female, could have 160 acres of government land after living on it for five years. As a result, people flocked to the northern plains, just as they had to Kansas. By 1888, at least fifteen farm families were arriving in Wyoming each day.

Cattlemen resented them from the start. Farmers, they claimed, were not real men. Men (meaning themselves) rode horses, carried six-shooters, and wore spurs. But these "homesteaders," or "nesters," walked behind plows and used "squaw tools"—rakes, hoes, spades. Worse, they had no respect for others' property. If a cow strayed into their fields, they saw no harm in butchering it for the dinner table. Ranchers traditionally "threw back"—that is, returned—cattle that strayed onto their range.

Nesters, however, were not the ranchers' only concern. The cowboy himself was becoming a problem. Smaller herds required

Ranchers now kept high-grade stock in fenced pasture and provided them with water from wells run by windmill power.

Farmers turned grazing land into fields of crops.

fewer workers, causing unemployment. In addition, many had lost their jobs after their outfits went broke in the die-up. Some sold their saddles, returned to Texas, and found other occupations. The cattle business had brought them little but misery. After years of hard work and danger, they had nothing to show but the clothes on their backs and a few dollars in their pockets. They resented the big ranchers, called "cattle barons," who had grown rich on their labor. As always, songs reflected their deepest concerns. By the 1890s these had taken on a bitter quality. According to one song:

> The cowboy's life is a dreary, dreary life,
> He's driven through the heat and cold;
> While the rich man's a-sleeping on a velvet couch,
> Dreaming of his silver and gold.

Another song urged parents to think of the future. Under no circumstances should they allow their sons to waste their lives with cattle:

> If you ever have a youngster
> And he wants to foller stock,
> The best thing you can do for him
> Is to brain him with a rock.

Or if rocks ain't very handy
You kin shove him down the well;
Do not let him be a cowboy,
For he's better off in hell.

The majority of unemployed cowboys remained in the North. Cowpunching was in their blood, and they could not imagine themselves doing anything else. But instead of looking for other jobs, they settled on government land and went into business on their own. They prospered. Within a short time, men who had begun with five or ten animals owned dozens, even hundreds.

That raised a problem of another sort. No matter how hard they worked, their herds could not have increased so rapidly by natural means. Nor could they afford to buy that much stock so quickly. There was just one explanation: The cowboy-nester was also a rustler. No farmer, let alone a townsman, could steal so many cattle and pass them off as his own. A rustler had to be an experienced cattle handler; in other words, a cowboy.

Rustlers stayed away from adult animals, since their markings made them easy to identify. It was better, and safer, to go after unbranded calves. But since calves stayed close to their mothers for almost a year, they had to be separated before the roundup. This could be done in various ways, all of them cruel. A calf's eyelid muscles might be cut to blind it until it got used to being away from its mother; the muscles healed after a while and the eyes returned to normal. Some rustlers slit calves' tongues so they could not suckle, or burned them between the toes to make walking painful. However, the surest way was also the quickest. The mother was shot and the calf given the thief's brand.

If a calf already wore a brand, it had to be altered. A rancher involved in rustling chose a brand that would blend with that of a large outfit nearby. This was done with a running iron, a rod with a slight curve at the end. The rustler heated the iron and then "ran" it over the original brand, changing it as needed. In this way an *O* became a *P*, a *P* a *B*, a *J* an *O*, an *F* an *E*, a *V* a *W*, an *S* an *8*, and so on. Nevertheless, a fellow could be too clever for his own good. Take the rustler who changed the

In this Remington drawing of 1887, cowboys argue over a brand.

I C brand to the I C U. All was well until the I C owner got wise and turned the tables. Within days, every cow on the range had a new brand: I C U 2. The rustler lost even his own animals but dared not complain.

One rustler was an artist. The X I T, the largest ranch in the Texas panhandle, had lost hundreds of cattle in a season. Its owners believed that cattle branded with the star cross, ✪, were actually their own. But try as they might, they could not show how their brand could have been altered. So they offered the suspected rustler five thousand dollars for his secret and a promise to leave their stock alone. He readily agreed. Each year, he explained, a certain number of calves were improperly branded, with the T "tumbling" to the right. That was all he needed to form a star cross, ⅄ǁ⅄ .[4]

Rustling was a crime punishable by a long prison term. Still, it was one thing to catch a thief, another to bring him to justice. In the North, small ranchers and farmers outnumbered the cattle barons, allowing them to elect county sheriffs and control local courts. No matter how much evidence was given, few juries would convict a cattle thief. Why should they? He was one of their own, a simple man struggling for a living against "them"—

the rich. *They* enclosed land and water with barbed wire. *They* resisted cowboy demands for higher wages. And when cowboys formed unions, *they* fired them as troublemakers. If a small rancher stole from a cattle baron, that was justice, in a jury's eyes. He was a Robin Hood, taking from the rich in order to live as a free man.

Large ranch owners saw things differently. They had held on after the die-up, taken risks, and invested in high-grade stock. They deserved their wealth. If the law would not help them, then too bad for the law. They would take matters into their own hands.

Vigilante groups were formed to deal with rustlers—permanently, if necessary. Suspected rustlers were warned to quit while they were ahead. A suspect might find a paper with a skull and crossbones and the numbers 3-7-77 tacked to his front door. These were the dimensions of a grave: 3 feet wide, 7 feet long, and 77 inches deep. Granville Stuart, however, was more direct. He formed the Montana Stranglers, killers who struck without warning. In a one-month period (July 1884), they shot or hung thirty rustlers. Finally, "range detectives," usually gunmen from the old Kansas cow towns, were hired to track down rustlers. They either took care of them quietly or gave their names to vigilante groups. Anyone found with a running iron was considered a rustler and dealt with accordingly.

Among the vigilantes' victims were Jim Averill and Ella Watson. The couple, who lived in the Sweetwater Valley of Wyoming, were not rustlers themselves. They didn't have to be. Ella, known locally as Cattle Kate, was a big, beefy woman of twenty-eight. She had several lovers, including rustlers, who gave her presents of stolen cattle. Ella and Jim ignored warnings to leave the Sweetwater. In July 1889, vigilantes hung them from a tree. No one was ever punished for the crime, and rustling continued without letup.

Wyoming's cattle barons decided on an all-out attack. Early in 1892, they sent an agent to Texas to hire men who could shoot straight and keep their mouths shut. The Texans would receive five dollars a day plus expenses, a generous wage in their line of work.

At four o'clock in the morning of April 6, a private train

Known as Cattle Kate, Ella Watson and her lover, Jim Averill, were lynched by Wyoming cattlemen who accused them of being rustlers.

halted outside Casper, Wyoming. Twenty-two Texans, along with thirty cattlemen and range detectives, stepped from the darkened cars. Without speaking, they unloaded horses, rifles, dynamite, and other gear. It was the best money could buy, since their employers wanted no slipups.

As the sun rose, they rode north toward Buffalo in Johnson County, one of the worst trouble spots. Major Frank Wolcott, a Civil War veteran and a wealthy rancher, led the column. In his pocket Wolcott had a list of seventy rustlers and their supporters, among them the county sheriff. There would be no arrests, no trials, no appeals to law. All were to be shot on sight.

The murder plan involved some of Wyoming's most respected citizens. In addition to the cattle barons, the state governor and both United States senators knew of the plan and approved of it. Even wealthy easterners were sympathetic. Later, after the plan's failure, the *New York Times* praised its leader's "wonderful determination."

Before reaching Buffalo, Major Wolcott learned that rustlers were at the KC Ranch. Since it was on their way anyhow, he decided to strike sooner than planned. At dawn, April 9, the invaders surrounded the ranch house, a one-room log cabin. Four men were inside: fur trappers Bill Walker and Ben Jones, and rustlers Nick Rae and Nate Champion. Champion, a Texan, was a real prize. He was thought to be the head of a large band of rustlers and also the best shot in Wyoming.

Shortly after daybreak Walker was captured as he went to a stream to get water. Moments later, they seized Jones as he came down the same path. Both men were questioned and later freed as innocent bystanders. Meantime, rifles were trained on the cabin door.

They did not have to wait long. When Rae went outside to call the trappers, they opened fire. Shrieking in pain, Rae toppled over, bleeding from wounds in his head and body. He would have been finished then and there, had his friend not come to the rescue. Suddenly the door flew open and Champion dashed out, a six-shooter in his hand. Bullets crashed into the door near his head, sending splinters flying. Champion ignored them. Instead, he dragged Rae inside with one hand, while returning fire with the other. A gunman, the Texas Kid, fell with a bullet in the leg.

Fifty to one is long odds, but Champion was a brave man fighting for his life. Hour after hour, rifle bullets poured into the cabin. Champion darted from window to window, firing with his six-shooter. Two more gunmen were wounded, warning the others to keep a respectable distance. By late afternoon, they decided that they had waited long enough. A wagon was loaded with firewood and hay, pushed up to the cabin, and set ablaze.

Strange as it may seem, Champion kept a diary of the battle. Now and then, when enemy fire slackened, he scribbled a few lines in a small notebook. Although he did not expect to survive, he wanted to leave a record of what happened and how he felt.

Here is some of what he wrote:

> It is about two hours since the first shot. Nick is still alive. They are still shooting and are still around the house. Boys, there is bullets coming in like hail. Them fellows is in such shape that I can't get back at them. They are shooting from the stable and river and back of the house. . . .

Later:

> Nick is dead. He died about nine o'clock. I see smoke down at the stable. I think they have fired it. I don't think they intend to let me get away this time. . . . Boys, I feel pretty lonesome just now. I wish there was someone here with me, so we could watch all sides at once. . . .

Later still:

> Well, they have just got through shelling the house like hail. I hear them splitting wood. I guess they are going to fire the house. I think I will make a break when night comes, if alive. Shooting again. I think they will fire the house this time. It's not night yet. The house is all fire. Goodbye, boys, if I never see you again.[5]

Flames enveloped the cabin's walls, spreading to the roof. Champion waited until the last moment, then grabbed a rifle and pistol and ran out the door. He had fired one shot when a bullet knocked the rifle out of his hands. While reaching for the pistol, twenty-eight bullets slammed into his body. The killers found the bloodstained diary in his shirt pocket. It was unimportant, to them, so they tossed it aside. As they turned to leave, someone placed a sign on Champion's chest. It read CATTLE THIEVES, BEWARE!

The invaders continued toward Buffalo. They were only a few miles away when they met a man who warned of danger. Local people had learned of the shoot-out. Small ranchers, rustlers, and farmers were gathering to avenge Nate Champion.

Major Wolcott led his men to the TA Ranch, fourteen miles from Buffalo, and prepared for a siege. It was now their turn to be outnumbered.

Three hundred men surrounded the ranch house and cut loose with rifles. They couldn't have been good shots, since no one on either side was seriously wounded. On the second day, they had loaded a wagon with dynamite and were pushing it toward the building when a bugle sounded. Just as in the movies, a squadron of U.S. Cavalry rode to the rescue with flags flying. Guiding them was one of Major Wolcott's men, who had slipped away during the night. The troopers broke the siege and took the invaders into custody. No trial was held, and all were eventually released.

Nevertheless, the "Johnson County War" brought people to their senses. The cattle barons realized they could not rule by gun law. Small ranchers understood that, to have peace, they had to respect their neighbors' property. Rustling continued, as it does today. But the worst was over by the spring of 1892.

The frontier cowboy had become history by then. The open range, trail driving, and cow towns were gone forever. As ranching changed, the cowboy devoted less time to cattle and more to gathering hay, greasing windmills, cleaning water tanks, digging postholes, stringing barbed wire, and mending fences. He still looked the same, except that he wore no six-shooter. Eventually all western states, including Texas, disarmed him by law. Although he might own a pistol, he could not wear it in public. Big ranches frowned upon weapons of any kind. The XIT Ranch was typical: No employee could have a six-shooter, bowie knife, slingshot, or brass knuckles. Finally, a new form of transportation appeared, early in the twentieth century. It was a homely contraption, rattling and bouncing and smoking its way across the plains. The smoke was so thick that an Indian, seeing it for the first time, called it a "skunk wagon." Old-timers still call automobiles "skunk wagons."

The man on horseback still exists, and will so long as people eat beef. Yet, for most people, he has turned into a legend, a hero who never was. The legend started in the East after the Civil War. Easterners lived in crowded cities, often working at dull, tedious jobs. People of all classes wanted more from life. They wanted color, adventure, and freedom in clean, beautiful surroundings. The cowboy seemed to have all that. He seemed a free spirit, a rugged outdoorsman who could do as he pleased, go where he pleased, when he pleased. And if anyone stood in his way—*bang!*

The Wild West show spread this image from coast to coast. In 1883, William F. Cody discovered there was more money in show business than in hunting and scouting. His show, Buffalo Bill's Wild West, was an instant success. Its posters invited people to see:

A COMPANY OF WILD WEST COWBOYS. THE REAL ROUGH RIDERS OF THE WORLD WHOSE DARING EXPLOITS HAVE MADE THEIR VERY NAMES SYNONYMOUS WITH DEEDS OF BRAVERY.

For just one thin dime, they could see trick riding, roping exhibitions, and mock battles between cowboys and Indians. Sitting Bull, who joined the show for a season, scowled at audiences; they loved being afraid of "Custer's killer." Annie Oakley gave them a thrill a minute. Sitting Bull called her *Watanya Cicilia,* "Little Sure Shot," a name she earned. Annie shot cigarettes out of men's mouths and coins from between their fingers. Using a shotgun, she once shot 4,772 out of 5,000 glass balls out of the air in nine hours.

Buffalo Bill's Wild West became the real West for millions of people. During a tour of England, one of his cowboys behaved as audiences had come to expect. He went to a fancy London restaurant and ordered a steak cooked rare. When it arrived at the table, he drew his pistol, shouted it was still alive, and pumped it full of lead. Another time, extra police had to patrol the docks to keep schoolboys from escaping to the Wild West.

The rodeo also featured cowboys as death-defying daredevils. We recall that vaqueros and cowboys were proud of their skills. During roundups, these were turned into contests between different outfits. Rodeos were held, and money bet, to decide the best rider, roper, and steer wrestler. In time, rodeos were held yearly in various western towns. Admission was charged and prizes offered, allowing performers to earn extra money. The first regular rodeo began in 1888 in Prescott, Arizona.

Blacks and whites competed as equals in the rodeo. In 1903, Bill Pickett, a black, invented bulldogging. Pickett would chase a longhorn, leap onto its back, and pull it down. He then would

Bill Pickett, a black cowboy, became a rodeo star. He invented bulldogging, throwing a steer to the ground by grabbing its horns and twisting its head.

Sitting Bull and Buffalo Bill. For a few months in 1885, "Custer's killer" was a leading attraction in Buffalo Bill's Wild West show.

bite the struggling animal on its lower lip and jerk it flat on the ground. Bulldogging is now a leading event in all rodeos.

Easterners could never get enough of western "lore." Cheap novels glorified killers like Wild Bill Hickok, Jesse James, and Billy the Kid. Countless magazines and newspapers carried articles and stories about "cowboy heroes." A magazine, *The Buffalo Bill Stories*, had weekly stories about his exploits. For five cents a copy, you could be thrilled by "Buffalo Bill and the

Silk Lasso" and "Buffalo Bill, the Wild West Duelist; or, The Girl Mascot of Moonlight Mine." Bill faced stiff competition from the likes of *Beadle's Half-Dime Library*. This series followed the adventures of "Arizona Joe," "Lariat Lil," "Fancy Frank, of Colorado," and "Denver Dan and His Band of Dead Shots." Needless to say, these stories contained not a grain of truth.

There are cases of boys running away from home after reading adventure stories. One was reported in the Cheyenne, Wyoming, *Democratic Leader*, February 1, 1885. Two detectives had come to Cheyenne in search of eleven-year-old Fred Shepard. The boy's father, a New York banker, was offering ten thousand dollars for his safe return. Fred, it seems, was addicted to western novels. The only clue to his whereabouts was the last novel he had read. It was found in his room, open to the place where a cowboy detective unmasks his father's murderer "and carves him into mincemeat . . . while holding the minor villains in subjection with two revolvers held in one hand." Scribbled at the bottom of the page was this note: "I'm goin' West to be a cowboy detective." Fred had taken twenty dollars from his piggy bank, climbed out a window, and bought a train ticket for the West. We do not know if he was ever found.[6]

The Old West became big business in the twentieth century. Railroads and automobiles, and later airplanes, brought swarms of tourists to "cow country." The eastern tenderfoot, his wallet bulging with greenbacks, found a warm welcome. Dude ranches allowed him to play cowboy in pleasant surroundings. Towns re-created their past to suit his notions of how things must have been. Dodge City's Boot Hill, for example, is a popular attraction. There is an annual Boot Hill festival, opened with an official song, "The Ballad of Boot Hill." Tourists can buy trinkets made in Hong Kong at a souvenir shop and wander among the headstones in the cemetery. But these are mock graves; the bodies were reburied elsewhere in 1879. Other towns have theme parks, featuring fistfights and gunfights, complete with tomato-soup blood.

Movies spread "the spirit of the West" worldwide. During the 1920s, cowboys went to Hollywood not only to appear in westerns, but in all sorts of films using riders. At $7.50 a day,

The Vigilantes Oath Organization by Olaf C. Seltzer
(Thomas Gilcrease Institute, Tulsa, Oklahoma)

Miss Annie Oakley—The Peerless Lady Wing-Shot, lithograph by
A. Hoen & Company
(Buffalo Bill Historical Center, Cody, Wyoming)

the pay was good, compared to ranch work. A few became stars. Tom Mix, a veteran of the Spanish-American War, had been a lawman in the Southwest. William S. Hart, a New Yorker by birth, had worked as a cowboy and had been caught in the middle of a gunfight between a sheriff and two outlaws.

These were the exceptions. Most cowboy stars were entertainers who took "western" names. John "Duke" Wayne was born Marion Michael Morrison in Iowa. Not only did Wayne star in a score of western movies, he was the hero of *John Wayne Adventure Comics.* William Boyd became Hopalong Cassidy and starred in sixty-six films plus a comic book series devoted to his "adventures." Roy Rogers, "king of the cowboys," was born Leonard Slye in Cincinnati, Ohio. He and others, like Gene Autry, were primarily singing cowboy actors and, later, comic book heroes. Their songs, written by professionals in New York and Hollywood, were sweet and sentimental. Most authentic cowboy songs did not have titles like "That Silver-Haired Daddy of Mine," "That Pioneer Mother of Mine," or "That Palomino Pal o' Mine." More often than not, they were rough and rowdy.

Western movies are not accurate pictures of the West. Cowboys are seldom shown at work, since that, apparently, is too boring for moviegoers. Movies feature fistfights and gun duels, which we know cowboys avoided. Stagecoach robberies are another theme. We see outlaws stopping coaches and holding up passengers at gunpoint and Indians chasing stagecoaches across the plains. But the Butterfield Overland Mail, the most famous stage line, was never held up and was attacked only once by Indians.

Television put the cowboy into every American home. Shows like "Gunsmoke," "Bonanza," "Rawhide," "Have Gun, Will Travel," "The Lone Ranger," and "Bat Masterson" ran for years. The cowboy's popularity made him an ideal salesman on television and elsewhere. Cowboys—that is, pretend-cowboys—have sold everything from beer and soda pop to laundry soap, flashlight batteries, barbecue sauce, peanut butter, underarm deodorant, and breakfast cereal. Until federal law ended cigarette advertising on television, the Marlboro Man pictured smokers as healthy, rugged western outdoorsmen.

The cowboy was no plastic figure, no cartoon character, but

a person with the full range of human abilities and failings. There were cowboy heroes and cowboy villains; mostly, cowboys were ordinary men, decent, hardworking, and good-natured.

That person, the *real* cowboy, survives. There are still those who ride horses and herd cattle for a living. Although they can find other work, they would rather do this than anything else. For them, as for us, the West still holds a magical attraction.

Some More Books

There are thousands of books on cowboys, Indians, and gunmen in the Old West. Here are a few I found most helpful in writing this book. Some are out of print but can be found in any large library. Although generally written for adult audiences, they are all enjoyable and well worth reading.

Abbott, E. C. "Teddy Blue," and Helena Huntington Smith. *We Pointed Them North: Recollections of a Cowpuncher.* Norman: University of Oklahoma Press, 1955.

Adams, Andy. *The Log of a Cowboy: A Narrative of the Old Trail Days.* Alexandria, Va.: Time-Life Books, 1980. A facsimile of the 1903 edition. This and Teddy Blue's book listed above are not-to-be-missed classics.

Adams, Ramon F., ed. *The Best of the American Cowboy.* Norman: University of Oklahoma Press, 1957. A valuable anthology.

————. *Burs under the Saddle: A Second Look at Books and Histories of the West.* Norman: University of Oklahoma Press, 1964. A lot of nonsense about the Old West, appearing even in "serious" books, is corrected here.

————. *Western Words: A Dictionary of the American West.* Norman: University of Oklahoma Press, 1968. A basic sourcebook, not only on cowboy speech but on the language of miners, railroad men, lumberjacks, and steamboat crews.

Ambrose, Stephen E. *Crazy Horse and Custer: The Parallel Lives of Two American Warriors.* Garden City, N.Y.: Doubleday, 1975.

Atherton, Lewis E. *The Cattle Kings*. Bloomington: University of Indiana Press, 1961.

Billington, Ray Allen, and Martin Ridge. *Westward Expansion: A History of the American Frontier*. New York: Macmillan, 1982.

Brown, Dee. *Bury My Heart at Wounded Knee: An Indian History of the American West*. New York: Holt, Rinehart, and Winston, 1970.

————. *Trail Driving Days*. New York: Ballantine, 1974.

Catlin, George. *North American Indians*. 1844. Reprint. New York: Penguin, 1989. A firsthand account of the Plains Indians during their golden age, and a real gem.

Connell, Evan S. *Son of the Morning Star: Custer and the Little Bighorn*. San Francisco: North Point Press, 1984.

Crosby, Alfred W., Jr. *The Columbian Exchange: Biological and Cultural Consequences of 1492*. Westport, Conn.: Greenwood Press, 1973.

Dana, Richard Henry. *Two Years before the Mast*. New York: Penguin, 1981.

Dary, David. *Cowboy Culture: A Saga of Five Centuries*. New York: Avon, 1981.

Dobie, J. Frank. *Cow People*. Boston: Little Brown, 1964.

————. *The Longhorns*. Boston: Little, Brown, 1941.

————. *On the Open Range*. Dallas: Ipshaw, 1931.

————. *Up the Trail from Texas*. New York: Random House, 1955.

Dodge, Richard Irving. *The Plains of the Great West and Their Inhabitants*. New York: Archer House, 1959. This book first appeared in 1876 and is a classic.

Drago, Harry Sinclair. *The Legend Makers: Tales of the Old-Time Peace Officers and Desperadoes of the Frontier*. New York: Dodd, Mead, 1975.

————. *Wild, Woolly and Wicked: A History of the Kansas Cow Towns and the Texas Cattle Trade*. New York: Clarkson N. Potter, 1960.

Dykstra, Robert R. *The Cattle Towns*. New York: Atheneum, 1976.

Faulk, Odie B. *Dodge City: The Most Western Town of All*. New York: Oxford University Press, 1977.

Fehrenbach, T. H. *Lone Star: A History of Texas and the Texans*. New York: Collier, 1980.

Fletcher, Baylis John. *Up the Trail in '79*. Norman: University of Oklahoma Press, 1967.

Forbis, William H. *The Cowboys*. Alexandria, Va.: Time-Life Books, 1973.

Frantz, Joe B., and Julian E. Choate, Jr. *The American Cowboy: The Myth and the Reality*. Norman: University of Oklahoma Press, 1955.

Gard, Wayne. *The Chisholm Trail*. Norman: University of Oklahoma Press, 1988.

———. *Frontier Justice*. Norman: University of Oklahoma Press, 1949.

———. *The Great Buffalo Hunt*. New York: Knopf, 1960.

———. *Rawhide Texas*. Norman: University of Oklahoma Press, 1965.

Hollon, E. Eugene. *Frontier Violence: Another Look*. New York: Oxford University Press, 1974.

Leckie, William H. *The Buffalo Soldiers: A Narrative of the Negro Cavalry in the West*. Norman: University of Oklahoma Press, 1967.

Limerick, Patricia Nelson. *The Legacy of Conquest: The Unbroken Past of the American West*. New York: Norton, 1988.

Lomax, John A., and Alan Lomax. *Cowboys Songs and Other Frontier Ballads*. New York: Macmillan, 1965.

Love, Nat. *The Life and Adventures of Nat Love by Himself*. New York: Arno, 1968. The autobiography of a black cowboy and rodeo star.

McCallum, Henry D., and Frances T. McCallum. *The Wire That Fenced the West*. Norman: University of Oklahoma Press, 1965.

McCoy, Joseph G. *Historic Sketches of the Cattle Trade of the West and Southwest*. 1874. Reprint. Glendale, Calif.: A. H. Clark, 1940. A basic source.

Mercer, A. S. *The Banditti of the Plains: Or, the Cattlemen's Invasion of Wyoming in 1892*. Norman: University of Oklahoma Press, 1987.

Morris, Edmund. *The Rise of Theodore Roosevelt*. New York: Ballantine, 1979.

Prassel, Frank Richard. *The Western Peace Officer: A Legacy of Law and Order*. Norman: University of Oklahoma Press, 1972.

Rickey, Don, Jr. *Forty Miles a Day on Beans and Hay: The Enlisted Soldier Fighting the Indian Wars*. Norman: University of Oklahoma Press, 1989.

Roe, Frank G. *The Indian and the Horse*. Norman: University of Oklahoma Press, 1955.

Roosevelt, Theodore. *An Autobiography*. New York: Scribners, 1923.

Rosa, Joseph G. *The Gunfighter: Man or Myth?* Norman: University of Oklahoma Press, 1969.

——. *They Called Him Wild Bill: The Life and Adventures of James Butler Hickok*. Norman: University of Oklahoma Press, 1964.

Ruxton, George Frederick. *Life in the Far West*. Norman: University of Oklahoma Press, 1951.

Schoenberger, Dale T. *The Gunfighters*. Caldwell, Idaho: The Caxton Printers, 1971.

Siringo, Charles A. *A Texas Cow Boy: Or, Fifteen Years on the Hurricane Deck of a Spanish Pony*. Alexandria, Va.: Time-Life Books, 1980. A facsimile of the 1885 edition.

Utley, Robert T. *Frontier Regulars: The United States Army and the Indian, 1860–1890*. New York: Macmillan, 1973.

Vestal, Stanley. *Dodge City: Queen of the Cow Towns*. London: Peter Nevill, 1955.

Wallace, Ernest, and E. Adamson Hoebel. *The Comanches: Lords of the South Plains*. Norman: University of Oklahoma Press, 1952.

Webb, Walter Prescott. *The Great Plains*. New York: Grosset and Dunlap, n.d. First published in 1931, this book is a classic and should not be missed.

——. *The Texas Rangers: A Century of Frontier Defense*. Boston: Houghton Mifflin, 1935.

Wellman, Paul I. *The Trampling Herd: The Story of the Cattle Range in America*. London: Fireside Press, n.d.

Westermeier, Clifford P., ed. *Trailing the Cowboy: His Life and Lore as Told by Frontier Journalists*. Westport, Conn.: Greenwood Press, 1978.

Weston, Jack. *The Real American Cowboy*. New York: New Amsterdam Press, 1986.

Whitman, S. E. *The Troopers: An Informal History of the Plains Cavalry, 1865–1890*. New York: Hastings House, 1962.

Notes

CHAPTER 1

1. Bartolomé de las Casas, *Very Brief Account of the Destruction of the Indies*, trans. by F. A. MacNutt (Cleveland, 1909), 314.
2. Quoted in Alfred W. Crosby, Jr., *The Columbian Exchange: Biological and Cultural Consequences of 1492* (Westport, Conn.: Greenwood Press, 1973), 88.
3. Crosby, 82.
4. Quoted in John Bakeless, *The Eyes of Discovery: America as Seen by the First Explorers* (Philadelphia: Lippincott, 1950), 94.
5. Quoted in Wayne Gard, *Rawhide Texas* (Norman: University of Oklahoma Press, 1965), 3.
6. George Catlin, *North American Indians* (New York: Penguin, 1989), 330.
7. Catlin, 327–328.
8. Richard Henry Dana, *Two Years before the Mast* (New York: Penguin, 1981), 131–132.
9. Quoted in David Dary, *Cowboy Culture: A Saga of Five Centuries* (New York: Avon, 1981), 65.

CHAPTER 2

1. The Louisiana Territory, claimed by the early French explorers, was defined as all lands drained by the Mississippi River.
2. Quoted in Wayne Gard, *The Chisholm Trail* (Norman: University of Oklahoma Press, 1988), 15–16.
3. Quoted in J. Frank Dobie, *The Longhorns* (Boston: Little, Brown, 1941), 15–17.
4. Quoted in Dobie, *The Longhorns*, 39.

5. Ulysses S. Grant, *Memoirs and Selected Letters* (New York: Library of America, 1990), 41.

6. Quoted in E. Eugene Hollon, *Frontier Violence: Another Look* (New York: Oxford University Press, 1974), 41.

7. Mrs. Samuel Maverick, quoted in T. H. Fehrenbach, *Lone Star: A History of Texas and the Texans* (New York: Collier, 1980), 458.

8. Most of the references to cowboy slang are from Ramon F. Adams, ed., *Western Words: A Dictionary of the American West* (Norman: University of Oklahoma Press, 1968).

9. Quoted in William H. Forbis, *The Cowboys* (Alexandria, Va.: Time-Life Books, 1973), 17.

CHAPTER 3

1. Quoted in Ramon F. Adams, ed., *The Best of the American Cowboy* (Norman: University of Oklahoma Press, 1957), 32.

2. A horse was always a "hoss" in cow country.

3. Quoted in Dary, 25.

4. Quoted in Hollon, 54.

5. Quoted in Richard Maxwell Brown, *Strain of Violence* (New York: Oxford University Press, 1975), 261.

6. Quoted in Stan Steiner, *The Ranchers: A Book of Generations* (New York, 1980), 65.

7. Quoted in Steiner, 65.

8. Quoted in Clifford P. Westermeier, ed., *Trailing the Cowboy* (Westport, Conn.: Greenwood Press, 1978), 101–103.

9. Quoted in Wayne Gard, *Frontier Justice* (Norman: University of Oklahoma Press, 1949), 202.

10. Quoted in Westermeier, 91–92.

11. Quoted in Adams, *Western Words*, 260.

12. Quoted in Forbis, 13.

13. Quoted in Dobie, *The Longhorns*, 94.

CHAPTER 4

1. Quoted in S. E. Whitman, *The Troopers: An Informal History of the Plains Calvary, 1865–1890* (New York: Hastings House, 1962), 17.

2. Paul I. Wellman, *The Trampling Herd: The Story of the Cattle Range in America* (London: Fireside Press, n.d.), 175–176.

3. Stanley Vestal, *Dodge City: Queen of the Cow Towns* (London: Peter Nevill, 1955), 60 ff.

4. Quoted in Adams, ed., *The Best of the American Cowboy*, 9–10.

5. Quoted in Gard, *The Chisholm Trail*, 167.

6. Quoted in Joanna L. Stratton, *Pioneer Women: Voices from the Kansas Frontier* (New York, 1982), 208.

7. Quoted in Gard, *Frontier Justice*, 258.

8. Quoted in Gard, *The Chisholm Trail*, 169.

9. Quoted in Harry Sinclair Drago, *Wild, Woolly, and Wicked: A History of*

the Kansas Cow Towns and the Texas Cattle Trade (New York: Clarkson N. Potter, 1960), 71.

10. Quoted in Gard, *The Chisholm Trail*, 168.
11. Quoted in Gard, *The Chisholm Trail*, 168.
12. Quoted in Joseph G. Rosa, *The Gunfighter: Man or Myth?* (Norman: University of Oklahoma Press, 1969), 168.
13. Hardin was arrested by the Texas Rangers and released in 1882, after fourteen years in prison. He wound up in El Paso, Texas, a rough border town. There, in 1895, he was shot in the back by a policeman out to make a name as a gunman.
14. Quoted in Dale T. Schoenberger, *The Gunfighters* (Caldwell, Idaho: Caxton Printers, 1971), 168.
15. Quoted in Wellman, 114 ff.
16. Quoted in Vestal, 23.
17. Ramon F. Adams, *Burs under the Saddle: A Second Look at Books and Histories of the West* (Norman: University of Oklahoma Press, 1964), 317–338.
18. Quoted in Clifford P. Westermeier, 54–55.
19. Robert R. Dykstra, *The Cattle Towns* (New York: Atheneum, 1976), 142–148.

CHAPTER 5

1. Quoted in A. Grove Day, *Coronado's Quest* (Westport, Conn.: Greenwood Press, 1981), 229–230.
2. Quoted in Bernard DeVoto, *Across the Wide Missouri* (Boston: Houghton, 1947), 41.
3. Quoted in Wayne Gard, *The Great Buffalo Hunt* (New York: Knopf, 1960), 24–25.
4. Quoted in DeVoto, 39.
5. Quoted in Otto Pflanze, *Bismarck and the Development of Germany* (Princeton: Princeton University Press, 1963), 472.
6. Quoted in Edward M. Coffmann, *The Old Army: A Portrait of the American Army in Peacetime, 1784–1898* (New York: Oxford University Press, 1986), 255.
7. Quoted in Gard, *The Great Buffalo Hunt*, 215.
8. Quoted in Daniel E. Sutherland, *The Expansion of Everyday Life, 1860–1876* (New York: Harper and Row, 1989), 25.
9. Quoted in Sutherland, 26.
10. Quoted in Richard O'Connor, *Sheridan the Incredible* (Indianapolis: Bobbs-Merrill, 1953), 339.

CHAPTER 6

1. Theodore Roosevelt, *An Autobiography* (New York: Scribners, 1923), 121–122.
2. Roosevelt, 127.
3. Quoted in Adams, *The Best of the American Cowboy*, 273.
4. J. Frank Dobie, *On the Open Range* (Dallas: Ipshaw, 1931), 181–182.

5. This and the rest of the story of the Johnson County War is taken from A. S. Mercer, *The Banditti of the Plains: Or, the Cattlemen's Invasion of Wyoming in 1892* (Norman: University of Oklahoma Press, 1987).
6. Westermeier, 336–337.

Index